CHAPTER ONE

WEDNESDAY 17 OCTOBER, 2001

HUNCHED in the passenger seat of a stolen car, Marcus Daniels glared out of the window as it made its way through the dark streets of Leeds. There were three others in the car, all armed and briefed on the task at hand. The car was quiet, each man taking a moment to themselves to reflect on their role.

Marcus observed the pistol in his hand, sliding out the magazine and checking it. It was fully loaded, but if it went well, he wouldn't need a single bullet. Sliding the magazine back into the gun, he took a deep breath and exhaled.

They had planned the job, and he and his team were ready.

The instructions had been simple. A drug deal was going down in Little London; Marcus had been ordered to ambush the meeting, steal the drugs and deliver them to his handler.

In theory, the job was simple, and what needed doing was clear, but it wasn't a job for one man. Marcus was smart enough to realise this. He'd gathered his younger team with this in mind.

This was their opportunity to prove themselves.

At the wheel was a younger kid named Frank. He was

eighteen, light-skinned with slight acne on his face, thin lips and large ears. Self-conscious about his skin, Frank wore a black beanie which he pulled so low it almost obscured his eyes.

'Can't wait to get paid, man,' said Killa-Billy from the backseat, breaking the silence. His face passed in and out of view as the car sped along, lit up by the dull streetlights lining the road. *Killa* was a seventeen-year-old Asian kid with a prominent forehead and sparse facial hair. His sense of self-confidence bordered on arrogance, which was curious considering his position. Despite this, he was always keen to prove himself, usually the first to step up if something needed handling. 'I'm going to Harvey Nicks tomorrow. Going to roll in with my tracksuit on and watch security tail me around the shop,' he said, a mischievous grin on his face.

'What are you buying?' Mace asked in his raspy voice. Mace was a chubby, brown-skinned man-child who was easy to get along with. He'd had a rough childhood; bullied persistently about his weight. When he decided he wouldn't take it anymore, things changed quickly. What started as a means to release anger and aggression became his weapon. What spare time Mace had was used practising combinations and power punches on a heavy bag. When those mentioning his weight were introduced to his devastating left hook, they soon stopped causing him a problem. Many of them became his friends.

Marcus had seen the potential in the group and had lured them in with promises of riches. If they proved to be as good as he thought they could be, they stood to make a lot of money together.

As an added incentive, Marcus had promised any additional money found at the spot could be split between them. He smirked as he listened to Billy, already spending the money before they'd completed the job.

'Need some jeans and a belt. You know how I do it. I'm

going to Notts at the weekend. There's that dance thing down there. It's going to be big!' Billy exclaimed.

'*Dance thing?* Tap or ballroom?' replied Mace, his cheeks wobbling as he chuckled to himself.

'Shut up! You know what I mean.' Mace composed himself before responding, a wide smile still planted on his face.

'Notts, did you say? I think I heard about that, actually. Yo, can I roll through with you?'

'It's a family thing, man. Can't do it.'

Deep frown lines spread across Mace's forehead as his smile vanished.

'Whatever then,' he said, as he kissed his teeth.

'Don't be like that, blood. We'll kick it next week.'

Shrugging his shoulders, Mace looked out of the window. 'Like I said. Whatever.'

'Why are you going on dodgy?' Billy frowned, annoyed at his friend's attitude.

'You're the one acting like you're ashamed to introduce your people to your family. It's cool to go robbing and take drugs with us, but when family are around, you wanna pretend we don't exist.'

'It's not even like that. We chill all the time, but you can't be bringing outsiders to family events. It's not the thing to do,' Billy defended himself.

'You two,' Marcus spoke for the first time, his voice low. Turning to face them, he looked from Billy to Mace and back again. 'Shut up,' he growled. He'd barely raised his voice, but the order was clear, and the two boys complied without question. Satisfied, Marcus resumed staring straight ahead. They were nearly there.

———

'Everyone knows what they need to do. We'll have the advantage when we go in strapped, but no shooting unless you don't have a choice. Do you understand?'

Each crew member nodded, their faces resolute. Marcus assessed each of them, hoping they were as calm as their faces implied. He needed people he could depend on, and this was their opportunity to prove their worth.

Frank swung the car left onto a side street and brought it to a stop on Oatland Close. They sat in silence for a moment, collectively observing the spot. The street was in the Little London area, located at the end of a maze of unimpressive, dreary-looking houses. It was the perfect place to do business, Marcus thought, as he analysed his surroundings. Nothing stood out, and it was relatively quiet by Little London's standards.

The eyes of the group were on Marcus, waiting for him to make his move.

'Drop us back a bit. Pull up in that lay-by behind us,' Marcus ordered. Frank complied, beginning to reverse the car. 'No, spin the car around,' he said firmly.

'So we're facing the way we came?'

Marcus nodded in response. One by one, the four-man team piled from the ride.

The meeting spot was a grey-bricked terraced house at the far end of the street. It blended in perfectly with the other houses around it, right down to the small, dirty brown gate and fence.

Marcus had surveyed the property earlier, so he knew the layout well. There were two entrances to the house, one at the front and one at the back. He and Frank would go in through the back, while Mace and Billy attacked from the front. If they timed it right, the dealers would be trapped, and it would be an easy score.

All eyes drifted to Marcus once more as the men waited for their orders. At well over six feet tall, Marcus towered over the others. His broad shoulders and muscular physique weren't just for show; he was deadly with his hands.

Securing his weapon in the waistband of his tracksuit bottoms, Marcus inclined his head, prompting Billy and Mace to move into position. Meeting Frank's eyes with his own, he nodded, and Frank followed suit. Though their identities were concealed with the masks the men had put on, Marcus's eyes flitted in all directions, alert and on the lookout for any signs of danger. The roads were quiet. It had been raining all day which had kept people inside. The deflated and dreary atmosphere was just the cover they needed.

Mace and Billy were in place, crouched outside the old wooden door that stood between them and the meet. Marcus and Frank hurried to the back.

Counting to twenty, Marcus kicked the back door hard below the lock. His aim was true, and the door burst open, the old frame splintering under the force of the blow.

Before he and Frank could move, gunfire erupted.

'What the fuck?' Marcus roared. He heard more shots, loud voices and then the unmistakable sound of Billy screaming. 'Hold up,' he commanded Frank. The youngster paused for a second, his eyes flicking between Marcus and the room where his friends were. Taking a deep breath, he raised his gun and charged ahead of Marcus.

'Frank, no!' Marcus called, but it was too late. Taking cover at the side of the door, Marcus grimaced as two more gunshots rang out. He heard them thud sickeningly into their target and a loud crash as a body fell to the floor.

Moving slowly, Marcus peered around the corner, confirming his suspicions. Frank lay splayed across a broken coffee table, motionless. Weapon in hand, Marcus dove into the room, avoiding most of the gunfire hurtling his way. A bullet grazed his left leg, drawing a grunt of pain from the man-mountain.

Rolling into position, Marcus listened for the footsteps of

his enemies. Popping up out of cover, he fired wildly, taking out one of the shooters. There were still three left, positioned around the room, preventing him from taking them all out at once.

Marcus needed to do something, and he needed to do it quickly. He looked to his left, his stomach lurching slightly at the sight of Frank's body. His eyes were open, but the mask obscured the rest of the kid's face. Placing his hands around Frank's ankle, Marcus pulled hard, dislodging Frank from the coffee table and pulling his body across bent metal and broken glass.

Marcus rummaged through Frank's pockets, grabbing the car keys just as the gunfire subsided.

'Daniels,' one of the shooters said, 'we know it's you. We've been waiting for ya! You've been had over. Your crew's dead. Kick the weapon towards us, and we won't kill you too.'

Marcus didn't reply, listening for background noise while the man spoke. He heard the subtle creak of feet tiptoeing across the room. The man wanted to distract him while his comrade snuck over for the easy kill.

Marcus wasn't going out like that.

Popping up again, he fired twice more, dropping the man attempting to flank him. Two down, two to go. They again opened fire, sending Marcus scrambling back to his cover.

Marcus was truly in a bind. He was running low on ammunition, and the police would undoubtedly have been called by now. If this was it for Marcus, he was determined not to go down without a fight.

Rising to his feet, his massive frame seemed to cast a shadow across the room. When his eyes found his opponents, he took aim and placed his finger on the trigger.

A frenzied cry from the front door captured the attention of the room. Mace had lurched to his feet, firing his gun

AMBUSH

wildly. He hit nothing, both gunmen immediately reacting and lighting him up.

Mace's sacrifice gave Marcus the precious seconds he needed. By the time the leader turned his gun back to Marcus, his friend was dead, and Marcus had his strap aimed at him. Marcus shot without hesitation. Once to the head and twice more to the chest.

The silence that followed was deafening. Marcus sighed as he looked around the room. Billy was sprawled by the door. Mace slumped against the far wall, his head lolled to the side. Frank was at his feet, his cheek almost touching Marcus's boot.

Moving his foot slowly, Marcus shook his head. Taking a deep breath, he bolted out of the front door and ran for the car. He needed to get away, before it was too late.

CHAPTER TWO

WESTY WAS fast asleep and snoring like a freight train when a slight creak disturbed his slumber. In his line of business, you had to be alert. His eyes immediately opened. Breathing deeply, he surveyed the room, smiling when his eyes settled on Chelsea, his long-term love. She was asleep next to him, her gentle breath a calming presence.

Westy groaned when he realised he needed the toilet. Sitting up and yawning, he stretched his arms before rising to his feet. A sudden movement caught his attention. With a yelp, he reared backwards onto the bed, smacking the back of his head painfully on the metal headboard.

'Did I disturb you?' growled Marcus Daniels. He loomed over Westy's bed, carrying something in his gloved hand. Westy wasn't sure what, but when the bedside light clicked on, his face paled.

Marcus gripped a claw hammer, his hands tightening around the handle. His breathing was steady, but it was clear he'd had a rough night. His clothes were torn, and a blood stain darkened the leg of his bottoms. Westy trembled as he looked into Marcus's eyes; bloodshot and tired looking, but wide and wired with murderous rage. He audibly gulped.

AMBUSH

'M-Marcus mate, what are you doing here?' Westy gibbered, trying to avoid waking Chelsea.

'I'm asking the questions. Who paid for the setup? The Yardies?'

'W-What setup? What are you talking about?'

Marcus sighed. Westy's eyes flashed once more to the gash on his leg. Returning his gaze to the man hovering above him, Westy searched hard for signs of pain, but found none.

Westy was small time in the streets of Leeds. He had made some money in the past selling drugs, but lost it almost as quickly as it came. Settling for something less volatile, he began using his contacts, working as a middleman, setting up deals and meets. He was in good shape for a man in his late thirties, with thinning dark brown hair and brown eyes.

Despite his impressive physique, he was significantly smaller than Marcus. His eyes flicked from the man to his phone on the bedside table, and back again.

'Don't fucking think about it,' Marcus said.

'Think about what?' Westy responded, feigning confusion. Marcus tilted his head to the side, his nostrils flaring.

'You must think I'm playing.' With no warning and astonishing speed, Marcus's left hand lashed across Westy's mouth. A gob of saliva flew out, landing squarely on Chelsea's forehead. Murmuring, she sleepily wiped the mess from her face without even opening her eyes. 'I'll ask again: who paid for the setup? I know you know. And you're going to tell me.'

'Marcus, c'mon, mate. Just tell me what's happened, and we'll sort it,' Westy wheedled.

Marcus's face tensed.

'I'm gonna break something, and then I'm gonna ask again.' He raised the hammer, and Westy screamed, jerking Chelsea awake.

'What the hell is going on?' she yelled. When she saw Marcus standing next to the bed, it was her turn to scream.

'Westy? What's going on?' she shrieked.

Marcus gazed blankly in her direction.

'Shut up, or I'll shut you up.'

Chelsea instantly closed her mouth, eyes dancing with fear.

'In fact, get out the bed. Now.'

Chelsea shot up. Shivering on her feet, she froze as Marcus advanced toward her. Grabbing her roughly by the back of her neck, he dragged Chelsea from the bedroom and tossed her into the bathroom.

'Stay in here. Make any noises, and I'll break your fucking jaw,' Marcus warned. He walked back to the bedroom just as Westy hurtled out of the door.

Westy was fast, but Marcus was faster. Blocking his path, Marcus hit him twice in the ribs with his free hand, folding the man. While Westy retched and heaved on the floor, Marcus brought his size thirteen foot down on Westy's back, driving the air out of him.

'My team got wiped out,' Marcus's tone was casual.

'I'm s-sorry to hear that, mate. I don't know anything about it. I swear I don't,' Westy moaned, quivering on the floor.

Marcus gripped the hammer a little tighter.

'Fine. If you're not talking, I'm not wasting my time.' He raised the tool, ready to bring it crashing down on Westy.

'No! Wait,' Westy screamed, waving his hands. 'It was Mori, all right?'

Marcus paused, the hammer still suspended in the air.

'Mori made you set me up . . . *Mori Welsh?*'

'He made me hire you, then had his men wait in the house,' Westy spluttered. 'He would have killed me if I didn't go along with it. Please don't hurt me.'

Marcus didn't even hear Westy's pathetic pleading. Of all the names he expected to hear, Mori's hadn't made the list. His jaw tightened, veins prominent in his overly muscular arms.

AMBUSH

Mori was a highly dangerous man, but he had made a fatal mistake in attempting Marcus's life. Soon enough, he would know exactly who he was dealing with.

'I'm keeping the ten bags you fronted me,' Marcus said finally, cutting across Westy's babble. 'Whatever number you've got for Mori, I want it,' Marcus said, throwing his mobile phone to Westy, who fumbled to catch it. Stepping to the bedroom shakily, Westy retrieved his phone. Eyes moving between the two phones, he punched numbers into Marcus's mobile before handing it to him.

'You bet on the wrong side, Westy.' Marcus said, stowing the phone away in his pocket. 'If I ever see you or that bitch again, you're both dead.'

―――

Mori Welsh paced back and forth in a safe house, enraged. It should have been easy to get Marcus. He had walked in blind, but survived. His carefully crafted plan had fallen to pieces, and Mori knew what that meant. There was a target on his head now, and one he would not easily shake.

'How the fuck did they miss?' he said, glaring at the other two in the room.

Deez, his blockheaded, muscled cousin, shrugged, looking sideways at Malston.

'Daniels got lucky,' said Malston. He stood resolute, puffing out his chest. Malston was an enforcer; a boxer in his youth who loved knocking people around. He had sharp features, besides his crooked nose that had been broken for some years.

'Lucky?' Mori repeated, incensed. 'You vouched for that team, Malston. You told me they were legit. That they could *handle business*. Well, they fucking didn't, did they?' Mori moved closer to Malston, who stood his ground.

'I've done jobs with them in the past. They never let me down,' he responded.

Shaking his head, Mori walked away, dropping onto the only chair in the room.

'Well, they have now, haven't they?' he said.

Malston didn't respond, the pair staring at each for what seemed an age.

'We know what Marcus is about,' said Deez, breaking the silence. 'There was always a chance he'd get the better of whoever we sent.'

Mori's eyes slowly traced from Malston to his cousin.

'So that's it then, is it? He's just some impenetrable fortress that we'll never be able to get at. Is that what you're saying?'

Again, Deez shrugged. 'I'm just saying there was always a risk. It wasn't a sure thing.'

Mori blew out a breath. Picking his gun up off the table, he closed his eyes and scratched his head with it.

'You need to understand, cuz, we'll never get more of a sure thing than we had. He didn't even take his proper team with him. Just a bunch of kids . . . and *his* fucking boys couldn't handle them.' Mori motioned to Malston.

Deez scratched his lip as he analysed the situation.

'But they were still affiliated with Marcus,' he finally said. 'Maybe the police will pick him up. We know they've found the bodies.'

'The police aren't going to get him. Marcus is a dumb idiot, but he rolls with Teflon, and Teflon isn't stupid. He'll keep Marcus out of prison, and Marcus will come after us. Not just Marcus, either. Shorty and his people will back him, and Marcus has other people he can call on.' Mori sighed again, rubbing his eyes. 'No, we're in this to the end. However it ends.

'Reach out to the usuals, pay them and get them on the squad. We'll use them as fodder against Marcus's people. Stay out of sight too—no running around partying or messing around with *little girls*. I want everyone underground. With a bit of luck, it might blow over.'

Even with his eyes closed, Mori could feel his team's stares boring into him.

'What is it?' he said.

Deez and Malston looked at one another.

'It's just . . . you seem really calm about all of this,' Deez said.

Mori opened his eyes and smiled at his cousin.

'Do you *want* me to lose my temper?' he said. Deez shook his head. 'Good. You've heard what I've said, anyway. You know what to do.'

With that, the pair nodded and left, leaving Mori to ponder his problems. Marcus would be after them, and Mori didn't want to give him an easy target. He wasn't scared of Marcus, but he respected his team's power.

Marcus had backing Mori couldn't match. Wisdom was useful, but he had his limitations. Teflon, on the other hand, was going from strength to strength. There were clear indications he would be the next major power in the city; the first person to threaten the likes of Delroy Williams and the Dunn family. Mori's success hinged heavily on whether Lamont would lend Marcus his support. Mori blew out a breath, placing his head in his hands. Feeling his phone vibrating in his pocket, he moved slowly, pulling it out and answering.

'Who's this?' he said.

'It's Erica,' the voice on the other end replied.

Closing his eyes, Mori sighed deeply.

'What do you want?'

'You know what I fucking want! Why have you been ignoring my calls? Why did I have to call you from a withheld number to get through to you?'

'There's some shit going on right now. I've been busy,' said Mori, leaning back and picking his teeth.

'*Busy* . . . You're always busy. I need money for your child, Mori. When are you coming round?'

Mori didn't immediately respond. Sitting forward in his seat, he glared off into the room.

'Who the fuck do you think you're talking to? Do you think you're going to get anything speaking to me like that?'

'I guess I'm lucky to be speaking to you at all, aren't I?' she responded.

'Listen,' Mori started, 'I'll give you money. But it's not for you and whatever addiction you're trying to work through at the minute. It's not for you to go out blowing it with your friends. It's for my son. If I get the faintest impression you're using any of the money I give you on yourself, I'll rip your fucking throat out in front of him.'

The silence was broken only by the increasingly heavy breaths coming from Erica.

'I'll drop by in a bit. Give you a bit of time to think about what I've said.'

Mori hung up the phone, throwing it to the side and reclining back in his seat. He loved his son more than anything, but his mother was a leach. He doubted whether a fraction of the money he had given her had gone to his son.

Walking into the kitchen, he carefully opened a cupboard that was hanging off the hinges. Extracting a large Tupperware box, he lifted the lid and grabbed a handful of cash, stuffing it in his pocket. Sighing deeply again, he walked to the door and left.

After visiting Westy, Marcus dumped the car he'd used and got a taxi home. It was still early in the day, and the sun was just rising above the tops of the houses.

Approaching his car, he paused before it, key in hand. Marcus looked longingly at his front door, wanting nothing

AMBUSH

more than to climb into bed with his partner, Georgia. Wiping the sleep out of his eye and unlocking his car, he climbed in and switched on the engine. He had business to attend to.

A little while later, Marcus arrived at Shorty's house. Switching the car off, he closed his eyes, took a deep breath and exited the car. Approaching the house, he could hear music thumping.

Checking his watch, his brow furrowed. His friend wasn't usually awake at this time. Marcus knocked on the door and waited patiently for a moment. When nobody answered, he turned the door handle, surprised when it clicked open.

As he entered the house, the music got louder. He closed the door behind him, taking a moment to survey the scene. The room was a mess. Alcohol and snacks littered the coffee table and much of the floor.

Marcus's eyes moved to the stairs. The music seemed to be coming from that direction. Moving slowly, he began making his way to the top.

The door to Shorty's room was closed, but not completely, a small gap visible. Moving quietly to the door, he placed his hand on it and pushed gently. When his eyes adjusted to the low light, a wry smile appeared on his face.

———

'THIS HOW YOU WANT IT?' Shorty grunted, as the sounds of two bodies slapped together audibly above the music.

'Yeah, just like that,' Stacey replied, her eyes closed, savouring the moment. They had been going at it all evening, Shorty more than equipped to deal with her insatiable appetite. Stacey moaned as Shorty worked her over, her light brown body seemingly melding to Shorty's.

Opening her eyes as the pleasure intensified, she dug her nails into Shorty's muscular back, pulling him in close to her, and placing her chin on his shoulder. Seeing a silhouette standing by the door, she screamed, pushing Shorty away and scrambling for the covers.

Shorty leapt to his feet without missing a beat, instinctively grabbing the gun he'd stashed under the pillow in a single motion. He pointed it at the intruder, ready to shoot.

'Put that fucking thing down,' Marcus said, stepping into the light.

'What?' Shorty asked, 'that or this?' he motioned from the gun to his groin.

'You know damn well what.' Marcus snapped.

'Blood, what are you doing here?' Shorty stared at his friend, unabashed by his nakedness. Like his namesake, he was short, stocky, with a powerful build he'd cultivated in his teenage years. He had short, closely cropped hair and skin the shade of a peanut shell.

'Come downstairs, and I'll tell you. And put some fucking clothes on.' Marcus headed downstairs. A minute later, Shorty heard the TV being turned on.

'I'll be back soon. Keep it warm for me,' Shorty said to Stacey. She sat up with the sheet covering her body, shaking, dark hair partially obscuring her face. Without another word, Shorty headed to the living room.

Marcus had his injured leg propped up on Shorty's coffee table, drinking from his friend's Hennessy bottle.

'I said put on some clothes. I don't need to be looking at your tattooed dick.'

'Shouldn't have turned up when I was handling business then,' Shorty fired back. Heading back to the bedroom, he emerged a few minutes later clad in a tracksuit. 'Now that I'm dressed, I'll ask again; what are you doing here?'

'Tonight went badly.' Marcus continued to drink the brandy.

'Badly how?'

'My team got licked. We got set up. They're all dead,' Marcus's voice was eerily calm.

AMBUSH

'You're joking! Vic's dead?' Shorty didn't believe it. He knew Marcus's guys, and they were good. Victor especially.

'Nah. The *B team* I was raising. The young guns.'

'Shit . . . Frank and them?' Shorty had seen the kids hanging around Marcus once or twice. They were raw but had potential.

'They were waiting for us at the meet. Opened fire as soon as we walked in the room.'

'That's a bit heavy for Westy, fam. He's a pussy,' Shorty said.

'It wasn't Westy. Mori was behind it.'

'Mori Welsh tried taking you out?'

Marcus nodded.

'And you're going after him?'

Marcus nodded again.

'Mori's real, you know . . .' Shorty frowned, scratching his head.

'So am I, Shorty. He started this, not me,' said Marcus.

'Mori works for Wisdom. Wisdom's big.'

'Blood, I know. I know Mori's real. I know that Wisdom is up there.' Marcus paused, glaring at Shorty, ensuring he had his full attention. 'You know why I'm here. Are you in, or not?'

The pair locked eyes for a moment. Reaching into his waistband, Shorty drew his gun.

'What the fuck do you think?'

Relief flooded Marcus, though he didn't show it. Shorty was mouthy, but skilled with a gun. Marcus needed his real team around him now. He planned to strike Mori. He just needed to work out how to do it.

'We've got work to do then. We need to track Mori and drop him quickly. Longer this plays out, the harder it'll be.'

'And Wisdom? What about him?'

Marcus scratched at his facial hair for a long moment.

'We need to speak to Tef about that. Ring him. Say we need a meeting.'

Shorty was already reaching for his phone. 'He's not gonna be happy. You know that, don't you?'

Marcus shrugged.

'When is he ever?'

CHAPTER THREE

AFTER ARRANGING to meet Lamont the following day, tiredness finally got the better of Marcus. Slapping hands with his friend and saying goodbye, he made for the door. Shorty, rubbing his hands together gleefully, bolted upstairs, removing his top halfway up.

The second Marcus closed the door and stepped onto the street, the music began thumping once more from Shorty's bedroom. Smirking back at the house, Marcus went on, jumping in his car, firing up the engine and pulling onto the road.

A short while later, Marcus pulled up alongside the curb outside his house. Balling his hands into fists, he rubbed his eyes furiously. Pulling down the sun visor, he slid the cover off the mirror and gave himself the once over. He looked a mess. His eyes were bloodshot and dark bags had formed beneath them.

Blowing out a breath, he slammed the visor back into position and removed the keys from the ignition.

Marcus slumped slowly to his door. Fumbling around in his pockets for his keys, he placed the key in the hole, relief washing over him when the lock clicked open. He was home, and his bed was waiting. Swinging the door open, Marcus stepped inside, kicking his shoes off and locking the door. When he turned back around, he was confronted by two piercing blue eyes, roving over him.

'Where the hell have you been?' Georgia demanded, her tumbling blonde hair swept over her shoulder. She looked equally as tired as Marcus.

Marcus and Georgia had been together for two years. He had met her on a night out and bought her a few drinks while they talked. They quickly hit it off. Marcus loved her with a fiery passion and knew she felt the same way.

'Hey, G. It's been a long night. I just wanna go to bed and sleep it off,' Marcus yawned.

'Oh, has it? And you think I slept well wondering where you were and what you were doing?' said Georgia, radiating fury.

'Don't start, Georgia. Not today.' Marcus hung up his coat and made for the stairs. Before he could reach them, Georgia cut him off. Placing her hand on his chest, she stepped back, looking Marcus up and down. When her eyes reached his leg, her mouth fell open.

'W-what happened? Marcus, why are you bleeding?' Georgia asked, tears pooling in her eyes.

'I'm not,' Marcus grunted. 'It's stopped.' He tried to step past her but, again, she stepped in front of him.

'You're hurt, Marcus. I've been up all night worrying about you. How long is it going to be like this? You coming home with parts of you missing and dismissing me when I ask about it? Who was it? What happened?'

'You know better than that, G,' Marcus responded, his nostrils flaring. 'You know who I am. You know what I do, and you know why we don't talk about my work.' Marcus waited a beat before continuing. 'Go on, why don't we talk about it?'

Georgia rolled her eyes and folded her arms petulantly.

AMBUSH

'I said, why don't we talk about it?' Marcus demanded, stepping closer to Georgia.

Georgia took a step back, surprised by the sudden shift in energy. Meeting her partner's eyes, she took a breath and responded through gritted teeth.

'To keep me safe.'

Marcus nodded slowly, stepping back and giving Georgia some room. The pair looked at each other for a moment, neither speaking. Finally, Marcus reached up and placed his hand on Georgia's cheek. Moving her face closer and placing her hand on his, she closed her eyes, enjoying his soft touch.

'I'm tired, G. I'm going to go up to bed. Are you coming?' he said.

Opening her eyes and smiling, Georgia nodded back. Taking her hand in his, Marcus led her up the stairs and into the bedroom.

Mori drove to Wisdom's house, unable to shake the edgy feeling that had overcome him. He had borrowed Malston's car, parking his in own in a private garage for now. He wasn't sure if Daniels or any of his team knew his motor, but figured it was better safe than sorry.

He'd needed the break from Malston and Deez. Malston's incessant justifications for the people he had chosen was frustrating Mori. They'd failed, regardless of their credentials. Deez seemed insistent on ignoring the situation, seemingly bored by what was going on, and waiting for action. As always, it would rely on Mori to rectify the situation, which infuriated him.

Beyond anything else, Mori was frustrated with himself. He'd messed up, and he needed to fix the issue before it spiralled out of control. He had his gun on him, wondering if word would have spread about the shootout. Shaking his head, he continued driving. He needed to deal with one problem at a time.

Mori approached his destination, a semi-detached house in a discreet location, not far from the Queen's Arms pub on Harrogate Road. He parked up, his eyes roaming over the location. The house was nice. It was an old build that had since been re-furbished, with large windows to the front, and a garden so neat it looked like a picture. An iron gate oversaw the property, and there were two cars parked in the driveway: a silver Mercedes and a large black Range Rover.

Mori knocked on the front door. A solidly built black man with a shaved head and sharp dark brown eyes stared out at him.

'What the hell are you doing here?' Wisdom asked. Mori looked at him for a moment.

'Obviously, I came here to see you.'

'You couldn't have sent a message first?' Wisdom said. Despite this, he stepped aside and let Mori in. They walked down a short, immaculate hallway. Despite not being fond of the quiet area, Mori was jealous of Wisdom's home. He'd been several times in the past, and liked the spacious rooms. He suspected Wisdom hadn't had much to do with the decorating, but he appreciated the modern, sprawling look regardless.

Wisdom led them into one of the two living rooms. It had a large, slim silver television, and several comfortable reclining leather chairs. The furniture was mostly dark brown, and the chocolate-coloured carpets were plush and high-end.

Ruby, Wisdom's partner, was curled up on one of the chairs, watching a film. When she looked up and saw Mori, she visibly froze.

'Babe, we're gonna talk in the other room,' said Wisdom. Ruby nodded, keeping her eyes on her partner. Mori's eyes roved over Ruby as Wisdom walked away. She was short and jam-packed with curves. She had curly, dark brown hair, hazel eyes and a thin face with full lips. Mori had a thing for her, and hadn't been shy in showing it. Flashing a grin and winking, Mori followed Wisdom.

'Why does your girl always act funny when I'm around?' Mori asked, as they sat in the second living room. This served as a pseudo-office for Wisdom. It had a sturdy light brown desk, several paintings of obscure landscapes on the walls, and two chairs on either side of the desk, one decidedly less comfortable than the other. Both men took their seats.

Wisdom shook his head.

'You're imagining things. It's not like you to turn up without a word. What's happened?'

'Have you heard about the shootings in Little London?'

'I know they found bodies. I don't know all of the details. Why?' Wisdom asked.

'Marcus was the target,' said Mori quietly. Wisdom tilted his head, frowning.

'As in Tall-Man?'

Mori nodded.

'What were you thinking?' Wisdom demanded, worry etched on his face.

Mori scratched his chin, taking a moment before responding.

'He's a problem, Wisdom. You know he is. I was trying to be the solution.'

Wisdom surveyed Mori for a moment before exhaling deeply. Closing his eyes, he began massaging his temples with his fingers.

'How did you come to that conclusion, Mori? We work with his people. This is going to cause all kinds of shit with Teflon.'

'Can't we handle whatever he throws at us? Are you doubting yourself, *boss?*'

Wisdom straightened up and glared at Mori. The pair had

known each other for years and, for all intents and purposes, Wisdom was Mori's boss. Wisdom was the brains of the operation. A numbers guy who cared about the money more than anything. He was all about business.

Mori was different. He liked to hurt people. For business, if needed, but for fun, if not. For a long time, the dynamic between the two worked well. They had carved out a nice path for themselves selling weed, pushing out many of the Yardies that controlled the market in their area.

When they had established a decent base, Wisdom implored Mori to fall back. To settle for what they had gained. Mori listened, but never forgot. It was an opportunity squandered, as far as he was concerned. A fact that Mori was quick to remind his boss of.

'It's not about what we can and can't handle. It's bad for business,' growled Wisdom through gritted teeth.

Mori rolled his eyes.

'Business, business, business. It's all you go on about. If you were so concerned about business, you would realise how much my move could have helped us.'

'And how do you work that out?' Wisdom replied incredulously.

'He's got a nice piece of the protection business. If I get him out of the way, I take over. *We* take over.'

Wisdom blew out a breath, shaking his head. 'You want to take out Marcus Daniels and muscle in on his business?' Mori nodded in response. Shaking his head again, Wisdom continued, 'I'm not sure you realise how fucking stupid that sounds. Just saying it out loud. I could barely keep a straight face.'

Mori's face hardened as he impaled his partner with a glare.

'Are you calling me stupid?'

'No, I'm not. Don't be daft,' said Wisdom.

'Oh, so I'm daft now?' Mori rose to his feet, taking several steps toward Wisdom. Mustering all his resolve, Wisdom stood too.

'What you've done is big, Mori. I don't think you understand the effects this could have. You're standing here trying to take offence at what I'm saying, but you got us into this shit. You're not daft, no. But what you've done isn't smart.'

The pair stood inches from one another, the tension palpable. Mori towered over Wisdom, but the smaller figure refused to take a step back.

After a moment, a small smile creased the corners of Mori's mouth. Turning slowly, he made his way back to his seat, and dropped into it. Wisdom did the same a moment later, draining his glass of brandy, before topping the glass back up.

'I hope you know what you're doing,' said Wisdom a moment later.

'Marcus isn't invincible. We nearly had him.'

'You should have handled it yourself,' Wisdom concluded matter-of-factly. Mori shrugged.

'I did my due diligence. Marcus was taking some kids on the move. It should have been easy, but they got cocky when they wiped his team out. They underestimated Marcus.'

'*You* underestimated him, you mean. If you forget for a second that he's a psycho, Marcus still has a ton of support. Teflon and his team are on the rise. You've seen how they handle people who cross them. You've put us right in the middle of their crosshairs.'

Wisdom waited for Mori to respond. When he didn't, he blew out a breath and continued.

'You don't get it, do you? There's a bigger picture here, Mori. There's always a bigger picture. Look at Blanka. They didn't struggle with him. There wasn't some long, drawn-out war of attrition. He shouted his mouth off, and then bang! He's dead. Murdered in his own spot. His crew knew who did it. Everyone did. Nobody went to battle for him. He was forgotten. Did you know his people now work for Teflon?' Mori folded his arms and nodded reluctantly. 'If they choose to come at us, what the hell can we do against them? We're not that strong yet.'

Mori snorted. Blanka had been a fool. He'd ran his mouth about taking out Lamont and his crew, and they'd set him up, turning his own people against him, and gunning him down in his living room. Despite numerous rumours about who'd killed him, the streets knew Lamont and his men were behind it.

Finally, he looked at Wisdom with disgust and replied.

'*Yet?* You're a fucking weed dealer. How can you ever match their money? Do you know what Teflon is making? You're constantly telling me to think about the future and to look at the bigger picture. Consolidating the protection racket could provide funds to close the gap on Teflon's crew.'

Wisdom let out an audible sigh. 'You can belittle what we've accomplished all you like. We live well. There was a time that would've been enough for both of us.'

Mori observed Wisdom for a moment. There was a sadness in his eyes that he hadn't noticed before. Mori couldn't question that his boss cared about him and their crew. He often disagreed with his approach, but his commitment was absolute.

'Are you my ally?' Mori asked simply.

Wisdom nodded. 'You know I am. But this is complicated. Teflon is our—'

'No buts, Wisdom. Are you my ally? Can I count on your support?'

Again, Wisdom nodded.

'So what are we going to do then?' Mori asked.

Wisdom stroked his chin, deep in thought.

'You were lucky to get the drop on Marcus. You might not get that chance again.'

AMBUSH

'Don't worry about that. I can get to him,' Mori responded.

'Good. See what you can do. I expect Teflon to reach out for a meeting. When he does, I'll attempt to play peacemaker. If you get your shot, take it. Friend or not, Teflon doesn't own Marcus. The protection business is his own. If we take him out, it's fair game.'

A sinister grin flashed across Mori's face before quickly subsiding. He had Wisdom just where he wanted him.

Wisdom worked closely with Teflon, and Mori couldn't be sure that his boss wouldn't play both sides. He was sceptical of his motives, but the deal had been made, and Mori was happy with the outcome.

'I best get to work then. You better stay out of the way for a while. Things are gonna get real messy.'

CHAPTER FOUR

AFTER A LONG AND RESTFUL SLEEP, Marcus woke up, refreshed and ready for the day. His first order of business was his meeting with Lamont, and he hoped it would set the foundations for their response to Mori.

He showered quickly, cleaning the wound on his leg with care, and wrapping a bandage tightly around it. Throwing on some clothes and making his way downstairs, he moved into the kitchen, opened the fridge door and grabbed an apple. Marcus bit into the apple, holding it in place with his teeth while hurriedly putting on his trainers. Returning the apple to his hand, he opened the door and left the house.

The meeting had been arranged at a small spot just outside the Hood. Marcus had been here once or twice before, and always felt secure when he visited. It was the perfect spot to meet. Relatively quiet and out of the way, they managed to avoid the scrutiny they often received in Chapeltown.

Climbing out of the car, Marcus looked left and right before making his way to the door.

As he entered the house, he took in the surroundings. It had barely changed over the years. Calling it minimalist would be an unwarranted compliment. The house was Spar-

AMBUSH

tan, its wooden floorboards devoid of gloss or varnish. Splintered in places and loose in others, people kept their shoes on to avoid unexpected injury. There was no furniture, except for an ugly brown sofa in the living room, which looked like it had been plucked from the street. Nobody sat in it, people preferring to mill around instead.

Marcus walked further into the house, nodding a greeting to those who noticed him. Seeing Shorty at the far end of the room, Marcus made his way over, slapping hands with his friend.

'What's happening, blood? How's the leg?' Shorty said.

'It's fine, don't worry about me,' Marcus responded. Looking around the room, he saw a tall figure leaning against the windowsill, looking out onto the street. His casual long-sleeved shirt clung tightly to his frame, and his combat trousers and black boots gave off a military vibe.

'What the fuck's he doing?' Marcus inclined his head toward the man.

'I don't know,' said Shorty, his eyes following Marcus's direction. 'Don't disturb his *Don Corleone* shit, though. We want him in a good mood.'

Marcus laughed, shaking his head.

'Nah, fuck all that. Yo, L,' he shouted. Every pair of eyes in the room cut to Marcus. All, but one.

Lamont Jones continued looking out of the window. After what seemed like an age, he turned around and smiled at his friends.

'How's the leg?' Lamont asked, making his way over to Shorty and Marcus.

'Fine,' Marcus replied, growing impatient. 'Why's everyone asking me? Do you think I've gone soft or something?'

'Nah. Shorty just told me you turned up at his house, bleeding all over his carpet.'

Marcus looked from Lamont to Shorty, his brow furrowed.

'If you weren't my boy, I'd have to debt you for that,' Shorty said.

'You could try,' replied Marcus, smirking.

'Let's get down to business,' Lamont started, the mood suddenly shifting. 'Shall we sit down?'

Shorty's nose wrinkled.

'I'm not sitting on that fucking thing,' he said.

'Guess we're standing then,' said Lamont.

Lamont turned to Marcus, motioning for him to speak. Marcus did. From the people he took on the job with him, to how it all went wrong, to his interrogation of Westy, he spared no detail. When he'd finished, he paused, took a deep breath, and looked at Lamont.

'Well?'

Lamont didn't immediately respond. He looked past his friends, deep in thought, scratching his chin.

'What if Westy was lying?' he finally asked.

'He wasn't lying,' Marcus replied irritably.

'How do you know?' Lamont's tone was mild, but Shorty could sense the frustration building in Marcus. His eyes flitted from one friend to the other, waiting for it to boil over. Taking another deep breath, Marcus spoke.

'Do you trust me?'

'Yes,' replied Lamont simply.

'Then take my word for it. Westy was telling the truth. I told you. I had a hammer to his head. Mori fucked up not doing the job himself. With or without you, he's going to get what's coming to him,' Marcus concluded, his words venomous. His shoulders rose and fell rapidly with each breath he took. Without noticing, his right hand had gripped the handle of the Beretta in his waistband, his finger hovering over the trigger.

Lamont noticed the movement, a flicker of disapproval crossing his face.

'It's deeper than that, Marcus. You know that. Mori works

for Wisdom. We do business together. You go chasing after Mori blasting that shit off, we're done.' Lamont motioned to the gun.

'Speak plainly, L. What are you trying to say?' Marcus's voice rose.

Lamont seemed immune to it, continuing.

'What you're talking about is bad for business. We've got something good going here, and I don't want you to jeopardise that. I know you're mad, but –'

'Mad?' Marcus demanded, cutting Lamont off. 'Mad, that his little pit bull tried to murder me? Yeah, I am a bit, actually. And you chatting shit about business and money is making me madder.' He seethed, nostrils flaring.

Lamont's calm rosewood eyes met his friends for a moment, the fire and fury easy to see. Visibly relaxing, Lamont looked to take control of the situation.

'I'm not saying it's not important, Marcus, and I'm not saying we should do nothing. I'm just saying we need to be smart about what we do. I'm not your enemy. Neither is Wisdom. Let me talk to him. Once I explain the situation, he'll help us.'

Marcus waited a moment before responding.

'What if he was behind it? Have you thought about that one? Or would that be *bad for business*, too?' Marcus snarled.

The temperature in the room chilled with Marcus's words. He and Lamont had clashed and argued in the past, but this was different. The silence stretched on for what seemed an age, the pair refusing to speak or move.

Looking from one to the other, Shorty considered how he could diffuse the situation. Only when the front door creaked open and slammed shut, did either man look away.

Making his way across the room, Xiyu Manderson, AKA Chink, moved merrily, a coffee container in each of his hands. Looking dapper in a dress shirt, trousers and breeches, he stopped in front of Lamont, smiled and held out one of the containers for his boss to take.

'Thanks,' said Lamont as he took the coffee.

'Where the fuck's ours?' asked Shorty, deep frown lines appearing on his forehead.

'I didn't even know you were here,' Chink responded, rolling his eyes.

'Don't roll your fucking eyes at me. You knew we were coming.'

Although Chink had been with the crew for a while, Shorty still struggled to trust him. When he and Lamont launched their drug line, they started small and, after some setbacks, their stock and influence catapulted them into a position of strength.

Lamont, now known as *Teflon*, made the big decisions and steered the ship. Shorty ran the streets, dealing with the runners and the distribution.

As far as Shorty was concerned, it worked well, and didn't need to change.

For a long time, Chink had wanted nothing to do with the hustle, but like many others, it eventually sucked him in. Dealing exclusively in the city centre, Chink built up a cocaine and ecstasy empire alongside Lamont, further enhancing the crew's status and reach. His business sense and financial acumen unsettled Shorty. It made Chink an asset in ways that he, himself, was not.

'Here, have this one,' Lamont said, thrusting the coffee container at Shorty.

'Nah, I don't even want it. It's not even about the coffee, it's the princable.'

'I think you mean, *principle*,' Chink responded, smirking.

Shorty's face contorted in fury. Pushing past Chink, he marched towards the door.

'Nah, fuck this. This meeting is over,' he said. Opening the door, he slammed it behind him.

AMBUSH

'Well, that was pleasant,' said Chink light-heartedly, smiling across at the door.

———

'You need to be careful,' Marcus said, as he and Chink exited the spot. 'One of these days Shorty is gonna throw you through a window.'

'I was messing around. I've never known somebody with a reputation like him be so sensitive,' Chink responded, looking across the street.

'Shorty isn't sensitive. He just doesn't like you,' said Marcus, grinning at him. Turning to Marcus, Chink returned the smile.

'Handsome, smart, well-dressed, what's not to like?' he retorted, popping his shirt collar.

Marcus smirked in response, flattening Chink's collar and pushing him into the garden.

'Come on, *Asian Cantona*, I've got something for you.'

Marcus walked purposefully across the garden, swinging the gate open and stepping onto the street. Chink followed in tow, a curious look on his face. Rounding his car, he took out his key, unlocking the boot and throwing it open.

Surveying his surroundings for a moment and ensuring the coast was clear, he lifted the false bottom, directing Chink to hold it in place. As he did, Marcus shifted the spare tyre and grabbed a duffel bag, dropping it on the floor.

When the tyre and false bottom were secured back in place, he bent down, picked up the bag and passed it to Chink.

'What's this?' Chink said?

'What I owe you. Seven G's,' Marcus responded. Chink opened the bag and looked inside. 'You gonna fucking count it or something?' asked Marcus, his brow furrowed.

'Nah nothing like that. It's just . . . is this from the job

Westy put you onto?' Marcus nodded. Looking back into the bag, Chink continued, 'taking it off you when you got stitched up and nearly died feels . . . wrong.'

'Who's being sensitive now?' Marcus smirked. 'I owe you it, take it. And don't worry about me. I still netted three grand for myself.'

Looking from his friend to the bag, Chink nodded, zipping it up and throwing it over his shoulder.

'Thanks, Marcus.'

'Nah, thank you. You helped me out when I was in a bind. I won't forget it,' said Marcus, smiling warmly. 'Let me walk you to your car. Make sure you get there safe.'

'I'm good, Marcus. I'm just a bit further on down the street.'

'Nah, if somebody sees you cutting about in those clothes around here, you're toast. Let's go.'

Chink remained rooted to the spot, looking at Marcus.

'C'mon, let's go,' Marcus repeated, nudging Chink. Losing his footing, Chink tripped into the metal gate, taking a moment to settle himself.

'Jesus, Marcus.'

'See,' Marcus responded, smiling, 'this is why you need me.'

The pair set off down the street, Chink clutching the duffel bag nervously under his arm. Looking left and right, his stomach knotted as he saw a curtain twitch, and a face disappear quickly behind it. Taking a deep breath, he held the bag closer.

'Relax, little man. Nothing's gonna happen when you're with me,' Marcus said.

'I'm average height,' Chink responded, feeling slightly burnt by Marcus's comment.

'That's a weird flex, bro,' said Marcus, chuckling to himself. Chink's frown deepened, a steely resolve appearing on his face. Doing his best to disguise a calming breath, he composed himself.

'We weren't all brought up on raw meat, Marcus. We can't all be nine-foot-two, or whatever the fuck you are. And besides, if you were as bulletproof as you're making out, you wouldn't have people trying to set you up and take you out, would you?' he replied.

Marcus stopped abruptly, Chink moving past him before he noticed. Facing Marcus, looking confused and slightly alarmed, he said, 'everything ok, bro?'

'Let's just get one thing straight,' Marcus started. 'We're cool, but you don't talk about my upbringing. You don't mention it, you don't ask me about it, you don't joke about it. Are we clear?'

Again, Chink frowned, wondering where the sudden shift in energy had come from. He was well within his rights to score a shot on Marcus, given how he was speaking to him.

Or so he thought.

Chink slowly nodded in response to his friend.

'I can't fucking hear you,' Marcus said, louder. 'Are we clear?'

'Yeah, Marcus, we're clear. Just chill,' Chink responded, worry etched on every inch of his face.

When Marcus set off again, Chink waited a moment before he followed. His face shifted quickly from concern to incredulity. Marcus had a tendency to go off with little warning, but given the circumstances, Chink believed he deserved more respect than his friend had shown him.

For a long time now, Marcus had been loaning money from Chink. Chink never asked questions or probed, and was never pushy about Marcus paying him back. Given how Marcus had blown up, Chink figured that now might be the time to change tact.

Moving at a slow jog, he caught up with Marcus's giant strides.

'Marcus, why do you — in fact, don't worry about it,' Chink said, shiftily glancing at Marcus.

'Why do I what?' Marcus responded, staring straight ahead.

'Nah, honestly, it's nothing. Don't worry about it,' said Chink, his eyes darting between the road and Marcus.

Again, he stopped in place.

'If you have a question, then fucking ask it,' he said, his eyebrows contracting.

'It's just,' Chink started, looking at the ground before meeting Marcus's eyes. 'You've been asking for a lot of money recently. Is–'

'Don't worry about it,' Marcus said, interrupting Chink. 'If your funds are low, I can get it elsewhere.'

'It's not that,' Chink replied quickly. 'It's just…'

'Just what?' Marcus replied, glaring at Chink out of the corner of his eye.

'Well, is everything . . . okay?' Chink asked, bringing himself to a stop this time. Marcus turned around, looking confused.

'What do you mean?' Course it is.' Marcus motioned to move, but Chink didn't comply. Standing firmly in place, he went on.

'It's just, like I said, you've been needing a lot of money recently,' Chink held his hand up when he saw Marcus ready to object, hurriedly continuing, 'and that's fine. I don't care about the money. But we see a lot of each other. I see the clothes you're wearing, the car you're riding around in. I know you're not into long-term investments or anything like that. You're not getting leaned on by anyone. Look at the size of you; nobody is leaning on a man who looks like you. So, in my mind, that leaves only a couple of options of what you're spending all this money on . . .' Chink let the statement hang in the air to permeate.

In truth, he couldn't be sure what Marcus was spending

his money on, but he had an idea. He watched as Marcus's face cycled through a whole range of emotions. From confusion, to anger, to frustration, to concern and, finally, sheer panic. Chink had never seen Marcus look so vulnerable.

'What are you saying, Chink? Are you calling me a fucking druggy or something?' Marcus said, gathering his composure and closing the distance on Chink in a heartbeat.

Looking up at his friend and meeting his eyes, Chink shook his head slowly.

'No, bro. I'm not saying anything. I just want you to know that I'm here for you. If there's something you're struggling with, you can confide in me.'

Marcus didn't respond. He stood for a moment, nose to nose with his friend, the pair breathing quickly. After a few moments, Marcus turned around, motioning to a car.

'Is this you,' he said, simply.

'Yep, this is me,' Chink responded.

'Cool. I think we're done here then,' said Marcus.

Knowing not to push things further, Chink nodded. Slapping hands with his friend, he threw the duffel bag in the back of the car. Pausing for a moment, he turned to Marcus.

'Mori,' he said.

'What about him?'

'Lamont has your best interests at heart, but there's a conflict of interest. He has to balance the business and his personal life, and that's tough. Maybe it's worth you speaking to someone who doesn't have a stake in all of this shit. Someone who can shoot straight and tell you what they think you should do.'

Taking a moment to consider his words, Marcus finally nodded in response. Nodding back, Chink climbed into his car and switched on the ignition.

As he pulled onto the road, he adjusted his rearview mirror, watching as the giant frame of Marcus faded into the distance.

RICKY BLACK

———

Heading back to the safe house, Marcus laid out a thick line of cocaine and snorted it, closing his eyes and savouring the moment. Grabbing a bottle of rum he'd left there earlier, he put on some music and relaxed, the thumping sounds of *MOP* keeping him in the moment.

The conversations with Chink and Lamont had annoyed him. They had their uses, but they overthought things, and Marcus felt it held him back. Sipping the harsh liquor straight from the bottle, he delved further into his feelings. Over the past few years, a wave of smarter criminals had taken centre stage, with Lamont at the forefront of them.

Marcus didn't fit that mould. He never would. Using his fists or a weapon was less complicated. He didn't have to talk to people and convince them to go his way when intimidating them was easier. In the past, Marcus had tried explaining that to Lamont, but his friend didn't see it the same way.

With the money he was making, he never would, Marcus mused. He sniffed another line, wiping his nose with his hand. There was a lot he needed to sort out, but he needed this right now. Plopping the liquor bottle on the coffee table, he pulled out his phone, looking at the number Westy had given him. Glaring at it for a long moment, he finally withheld his number and dialled.

'Yeah?' A voice Marcus recognised as Mori's answered. He didn't immediately respond, considering how calm Mori sounded.

'Oi, who's this?' Mori snapped.

'Your people missed,' said Marcus, knowing Mori would understand. There was a moment's pause before he replied.

'Shit happens, Tall-Man. It won't happen again, though. Believe that.'

'You're a pussy,' Marcus growled, immediately annoyed.

AMBUSH

'That's why you didn't come for me. You could never step to me man-to-man, you little punk.'

'Whatever. We took out your shitty little team, and we're coming for you too,' said Mori, before hanging up.

Marcus called back, but the call went straight to voicemail. After trying again, Marcus threw the phone down, breathing hard. He wasn't sure what he'd expected to accomplish. He hadn't expected to get under Mori's skin, but he'd needed to hear him, to make it all seem real.

Preparing a third line, Marcus sniffed it, straightening up, his eyes wide and wild. He would get to Mori before Mori got to him, that much he knew.

CHAPTER FIVE

THE FOLLOWING AFTERNOON, Victor drove Marcus home. He was edgy from staying up late, unable to switch off after his drug-fuelled conversation with Mori. It was as if hearing the man's voice had flicked a switch in his mind. Images of Mori plagued Marcus; walking around and shouting his mouth off about taking his team out. Only a few more lines and more liquor had helped Marcus pull through.

As Victor pulled up to Marcus's place, Marcus winced, his head pounding. He'd had a killer headache since waking up, and had only logged a few hours sleep. He'd done some working out, trying to burn off excess energy, but still felt wired.

'Wait here,' he said to Victor, climbing out of the ride. Marcus ensured his gun was within reach, glancing up and down the street. The cold winter wind blowing created an eerie feeling. Even mid-afternoon, it sent a chill straight to Marcus's bones, and he hurried to get inside.

As soon as he entered, he heard a flurry of steps, Georgia approaching hurriedly and flinging her arms around him.

'Where were you, Marcus?' She asked, her words muffled as her head pushed against his chest. Pulling away, she looked at him, tears in her blue eyes. 'Do you know how worried I was?'

'I'm fine, G,' said Marcus. Georgia shook her head.

'The last time I saw you, you were covered in blood, telling me you couldn't talk about it. What am I supposed to think?' Not waiting for an answer, Georgia examined his face. 'You look wrecked.'

Marcus shook his head.

'I'm fine. Just need to sleep.'

'Marcus . . .' Georgia sighed. 'I know you can't talk to me about whatever's going on, but maybe we need to get away for a bit? I've got some time off saved at work. We could go —'

'Not right now,' Marcus interrupted. His tone softened when he saw her face fall. 'I'm sorry. There's a lot going on, though. I can't get away right now, but I'm gonna fix this. For now, you need to go and see Angie for a bit.'

'Why?' Georgia made a face. 'Why would I need to see my sister?'

Marcus scratched his chin, still watching her. It wouldn't be an easy sell, but he needed to push ahead.

'You need to go and stay with her for a bit. Until this shit blows over.'

'What?' Georgia gasped. 'No. This is my house. I'm not going anywhere. You can't even tell me what's going on.'

'Yes, for your own good,' Marcus pointed out. 'I don't wanna argue with you, but you might not be safe here. That's all I can say. I need to handle the situation, but I can't do it if I'm worrying about you being here without protection.'

'Marcus . . .'

'No,' he replied. 'This isn't up for negotiation. You need to do this. I'll get you back here as soon as I can, but you need to get your stuff together. Now.'

Georgia stared at Marcus, a range of emotions playing across her face. Her blue eyes grew cold as she turned on her heel and flounced away, storming upstairs. Rubbing his forehead, Marcus went to make a coffee, needing the boost.

Before long, Georgia had her suitcase. Making her way down the steps, she dragged the case, letting it bang loudly on each step. Marcus ignored the petulant protest, picking it up and carrying it to the car. When they were set, Georgia climbed in the back, and Marcus sat next to her.

'Hello, Vic,' Georgia said to the driver, who responded. She shot Marcus a dark look, folding her arms as they drove away.

It didn't take long to get to Angie's, but the tension didn't ease. The closer they got, the colder Georgia grew. Angie lived on the outskirts of Pudsey, and had a quaint little house with a bright red door. It was the perfect family home, yet she had nobody to share it with.

They climbed from the car. Marcus grabbed Georgia's things and led her to the house. Waiting for Angie to answer, he tilted Georgia's head so she was looking at him.

'It won't be for long. I promise.'

Georgia looked back at Marcus, but said nothing.

That evening, Marcus awoke from a nap, yawning and stretching. After dropping off Georgia and checking in with Shorty, he'd headed back to his main safe house. He didn't want to stay at his and Georgia's place and draw more attention to it than necessary, but planned to send Sharma to pick up some clothes and other essentials for him soon.

If his current safe house became compromised, he had another spot ready that he could go to, but doubted he would need it. Marcus and the others had carefully picked their spots, and they were well-protected and out of the way.

Heading to the bathroom, Marcus washed his face and freshened up, debating sending Georgia a text message. He had some making up to do, but it would have to wait for now.

There wasn't much food in the safe house — something else he would need to have his men rectify — but Marcus prepared some instant noodles, devouring them along with several slices of bread. After drinking a few glasses of water, he grabbed his jacket and gloves and left, making a phone call as he did so.

The cold air hit him again when he was outside, but he was equal to it this time, not letting the biting wind bother him. Climbing into his car, he drove away, his gun within reach on the passenger seat.

Marcus arrived at Jukie's, swinging open the door and heading to the bar. Those who chanced a glance at Marcus quickly averted their gaze.

After ordering two beers, Marcus surveyed the area, looking for the man he was meeting. When he spotted him, he made his way across, placing the beer in front of him and taking the seat opposite.

'Thanks,' said Lennox Thompson, picking up the bottle and taking a sip.

Lennox was two years older than Marcus, and the pair had worked together in the past. His reputation was impeccable; a cold, calculated and methodical operator who commanded the utmost respect. His line of work was curious, given the climate in Chapeltown. He was ardently anti-drug, but why, Marcus did not know. Regardless, it added to the sense of mystique and reputation he had cultivated.

'Heard you've got a little problem,' Lennox said.

'What the fuck is Mori playing at?' Marcus responded, cutting to the chase.

'Can you honestly say you're surprised? Mori is tapped in the head. I've put out the feelers. Nobody seems to know why he did it.' Lennox scratched his chin, deep in thought. 'Talk me through how it went down.'

Marcus broke down the situation, explaining how they had been ambushed at the job, and how his team had been wiped out.

It struck Marcus that it was the first time since the event that he had truly considered them. They were young and had their whole lives ahead of them. They knew the risks when they signed up, but that didn't excuse the loss of life. For a moment, Marcus pondered whether their fate was inevitable when they'd signed up with him.

Pushing away the thoughts, he concluded his story and waited for Lennox to respond.

'Did you recognise any of the crew he sent after you?'

Marcus shook his head. 'I think they were free-lance. I've seen a few of his team around, and none of them fit the description.'

'Did you get a good look at them?' Lennox responded, his eyebrows raised.

'What do you mean? Course I did,' said Marcus, frowning.

'You seem to be forgetting, I've seen what you do to people's faces,' said Lennox, a sinister grin on his face.

Marcus smirked back.

'True. But no, there was no time for fun. I was scrambling.'

'What about Wisdom? Do you think he's got the balls to be involved with something like this?'

Marcus did. He didn't like Wisdom and was sure the feeling was mutual. Wisdom was connected with people Marcus had had disagreements with in the past. He'd heard rumours about Wisdom funding them, but had no tangible evidence.

'I'm not sure about balls. He's certainly dumb enough. I can't think why he would, though. He knows what would happen if he hit me. Why would he take that risk?'

Lennox scratched his head, cagey as always. Marcus had noticed that about him. He preferred listening to speaking, and his long silences often unnerved people.

AMBUSH

'You need to start taking out his team,' Lennox responded. 'It might be worth speaking to Westy again. See if there's anything he didn't tell you before.'

Marcus nodded. 'I was planning on finding him tomorrow. I know Mori has a guy called *Deez* he keeps close. Then there's a couple of others I know by sight.'

Lennox gave Marcus a knowing glance.

'Is L rolling with you on this one?'

Marcus shrugged. 'L and Wisdom are cool. He didn't seem too keen on taking sides when we spoke.'

Lennox's eyebrows rose. 'You and L are like brothers. That surprises me. I've no doubt he will ride out with you if it comes to it, though.'

'L's a businessman; he's not a soldier.' Marcus responded.

'I think you underestimate him,' said Lennox. 'L is a thinker. Do you know how rare that is in your game? You can't always shoot first and ask questions later. Lamont is cold and calculating. I think he will surprise you. He will make the right choices, exactly when they need to be made.'

Marcus was surprised. Rarely did Lennox speak of others with such reverence.

'Sounds like you have a lot of respect for him,' he said.

'He intrigues me. L shouldn't fit in our world, yet he's perfect for it. It'll be interesting to see where the path leads him,' Lennox said, staring off into the distance.

'You think he can go that far?' Lennox waited a moment before meeting Marcus's eyes.

'There are some questions he has to answer. He has to prove himself in some ways. The key to what Lamont achieves is in himself. Can he be ruthless when the time comes?'

Marcus considered the question for a moment before responding.

'I think he's got it in him,' he admitted.

Lennox grinned.

'So do I.' He checked his watch and stood up. 'I've got to go and see someone. Think about what I've said. You'll be alright.'

'Keep me posted if you hear anything,' Marcus said, standing himself.

'I will. If you need backup, then let me know. I'm with you.'

'I appreciate that,' replied Marcus, and he truly did. With Lamont on the fence about helping him, he needed allies.

When Lennox left, Marcus had another drink, appreciating the atmosphere. He could see people slyly watching him, assuming several of them would be running to Mori to report on his meeting. Marcus didn't care. If Mori was stupid enough to run up in Jukie's, Marcus would be the least of his worries. Jukie was well-respected, and his establishment was neutral ground. It was a fact that was very rarely tested.

Deciding to call it a night, Marcus clambered to his feet, just as a man hailed him.

'Daniels.'

Marcus glanced up, noting a square-jawed, light-skinned man with hard dark eyes and thin lips. Marcus nodded at Sheldon.

'You on duty?' He asked, looking the officer up and down. Sheldon shook his head. He was a year older than Marcus, and had been a Police constable for almost two years. He'd been training since Marcus last saw him. His shoulders and arms seemed to have broadened, evident even through the hooded top and body warmer combination he wore. His goatee was trimmed neatly, and he had very little facial hair.

Sheldon had surprised a lot of people when he joined the police force, but as he treated people fairly and consistently, it was rarely held against him.

'I wouldn't be in here if I was on duty,' Sheldon replied. Marcus shrugged. He sat back down, signalling for Sheldon to follow suit.

AMBUSH

'What would your colleagues think of you slumming it in the Hood with the bandits?' He asked.

'I grew up around here. Don't forget that, bro,' said Sheldon. 'Look, I'll skip the preamble. I heard about your crew.'

Marcus inwardly tensed, but said nothing, waiting Sheldon out. Clearly expecting this, Sheldon nodded.

'A few of my colleagues think you're involved. A bunch of kids going out to Little London, getting killed. Bodies all over the place . . . it doesn't look good.'

'I don't know what you're talking about,' said Marcus quietly. Sheldon shook his head.

'This isn't that kind of chat, Marcus. I'm just trying to warn you. People think you're involved, so just be careful. There's a lot of eyes on the Hood right now. We go way back, and you've always done right by me, so I'm giving you the score.'

Rising to his feet, Marcus signalled to the bartender, who hurried over.

'Get him what he wants, and get me another Red Stripe,' said Marcus. Sheldon thanked him, ordering a drink. They made small talk for a few minutes about football, which Marcus contributed to, and about the streets, which he did not. Draining the last of his beer, Marcus nodded to the officer and left.

Outside, he analysed the conversations he'd had. Other than his words about Lamont, Lennox hadn't said much that Marcus didn't already know. Sheldon's warning was appreciated, but not necessary. Marcus wouldn't allow himself to be caught out by the police, and would put the word out to ensure his team watched their backs.

Pulling out his phone, he texted Shorty, telling him to meet him at one of the spots. They needed a plan of action.

CHAPTER SIX

THE NEXT MORNING, the pair sat slumped on the sofa in a run-down spot. The air was heavy with the smell of damp, musty wallpaper. Cracks ran up the flaking walls like spiderwebs. A ragged, threadbare carpet stretched out beneath their feet. The faded sofa had been worn thin by years of use, the sagging cushions offering little comfort. They needed a quiet place to think and strategise, but the time they had spent had yielded little.

Shorty, perched on the edge of the sofa, clutched his energy drink in one hand. His other hand rested on his forehead, his elbow digging into his thigh. Marcus was reclining in his seat alongside him, staring up at the roof, his hands on his head.

It had been a long night, fuelled by caffeine, takeaway food and, when Marcus could slip away to his car, his magic white powder. The longer the night went on, the more appealing it became to him. His mind drifted to his glove compartment as he and Shorty struggled to put together a cohesive plan. Now it was morning, and his head was a mess. The sun was penetrating the moth-eaten curtains, the glare blinding.

AMBUSH

'I'm fucking thirsty,' Marcus said, his voice hoarse. 'Do we have anything to drink besides those energy drinks?'

'Nah,' Shorty responded, holding up a carrier bag. 'We've got plenty of these, though.' Placing the carrier bag on the floor, he removed one of the drinks from the packaging, cracked it open and handed it to his friend. Marcus took a long drink, wincing slightly as he did.

'It's warm,' he said, pulling a face and looking at the can in disgust.

'What do you expect? It's not like we've got a fridge here,' said Shorty. Taking another liberal swig, Marcus grimaced. Leaning forward, he swiped the crumpled cans and empty takeaway boxes onto the floor, placing his can where the items had vacated.

Shorty looked from the floor to Marcus, but said nothing

'Have you heard from K-Bar this morning?' Marcus said, still focusing on the can in front of him.

'Nah, I haven't. He'll be out there looking, though. Don't worry about that. My guy's legit,' Shorty responded.

Marcus nodded his approval.

'L still hasn't reached out. What do you think he's up to?'

Shorty waited a beat before responding.

'Probably still speaking to Wisdom. Trying to make sense of what's happened.'

Again, Marcus nodded.

'That was my thinking too. Don't expect we'll hear from him again until he's comfortable he has as much info as he can get.'

Marcus laid back in his seat once more, taking a deep breath and massaging his temples. He had known Lamont for a long time, and he, more than anybody else, knew how he liked to operate. He would use his contacts as leverage for information before formulating a plan.

This situation seemed different.

As far as Marcus was concerned, there was a possibility

Wisdom was involved in what happened. For all Marcus knew, Wisdom was the one who'd wanted him dead.

Closing his eyes for a moment, Marcus considered the situation he was in. For a long time, he'd seemed untouchable. The man to go to if you had a problem. The person whose silhouette you didn't want to see approaching you in a dark alley. Mori had damaged this perception and would pay for it.

His mind continued to drift, his head beginning to drop to the side.

'Fucking hell, man. I'm knackered,' said Shorty, stretching and yawning loudly.

Marcus's eyes snapped open. Checking the screen of a nearby Nokia 8210 to see if anyone had called, Shorty continued, 'can't believe no one's reported in yet.'

Marcus rubbed his eyes, his head pounding. With every thump of pain in his temple, his mood worsened. He didn't like sitting around and planning. He was a man of action.

'We need to do summat instead of just sitting here waiting for people to call us. What the fuck are we?' Marcus said, leaving the question to linger for a moment. 'Are we little bitches who are gonna sit holed up here all day? Nah, fuck that. We need to make a move.'

Shorty watched as Marcus rose to his feet and began pacing the room, seemingly unaware of the cartons and cans he was kicking around.

'What are we gonna do?' Shorty replied. 'We don't even know who Mori's people are. Other than Deez, we know nothing. We know faces, but no names. Do you wanna draw pictures of them to flash around to people and hope they know who we're on about?'

Marcus stopped on the spot, impaling Shorty with a glare. After a moment, he continued pacing.

'Listen, Marcus. We both know Mori is a snakey bastard. He's ripped off most of the people he's worked with. If it

AMBUSH

wasn't for Wisdom, he would be on his own. We need to know what we're dealing with, though.'

Marcus took a second to look at his friend. It was uncomfortable hearing him be the voice of reason. Taking a deep breath, he spoke, 'I know. It's just sitting around here is making me feel weak. I want the little prick's neck in my hands,' he said, holding his hands out in front of him with a wild look in his eyes.

Before Shorty could reply, there was a loud knock at the door. Shorty jumped to his feet, both men alert, their guns raised.

'You tell anyone we were here?' Marcus whispered to Shorty, his eyes fixed firmly on the door.

'No. Did you?'

Marcus shook his head, slowly approaching the door and signalling for Shorty to cover him.

'Who the fuck is it?' he called out.

'A friend,' a familiar voice said.

Confused, Marcus opened the door, standing aside as Chink sauntered into the room, holding a bottle of water in one hand and a phone in the other. He wore a neat sweater, Gore-Tex trousers and brown boots, and looked refreshed compared with Marcus and Shorty.

'What are you doing here?' Shorty asked, not even bothering to hide the dislike in his voice.

'Did L send you?' Marcus followed up.

Chink took his time responding. He took a liberal sip of water, his eyes taking in everything in the room.

'Have you two been up all night?' he finally said.

'Fuck that. Why are you here?' Shorty snapped.

Again, Chink ignored him.

'You need to sleep. You can't function if you're tired.'

'That's what God invented energy drinks for. Don't worry about us. We know how to do this. Why are you here? Don't pretend you didn't hear me.' Shorty's voice rose, rapidly approaching his snapping point. Marcus recognised the signs, and he knew Chink did too.

'I'm here to help. I know L's working with Wisdom, but I had a feeling you two might do your own thing,' Chink explained. Finishing the bottle of water, he laid it down on the table.

'So what now? You going to tell L that we're in here plotting?' Shorty demanded.

'No. As I said, I'm here to help,' Chink's tone was still calm. He wasn't intimidated by Shorty, and Marcus could tell it bothered the stocky thug.

'How can you help?' Marcus asked, his tone less hostile than Shorty's.

'Having somebody to plan with who's had a full night's sleep is probably a good start,' said Chink. 'What have you got so far?'

Marcus looked across at Shorty, who slumped back onto the sofa, folding his arms.

'Not much, honestly,' Marcus admitted. 'We've had K-Bar and his lot out there trying to find stuff on Mori. The only person we know by name that rolls with him is Deez. We don't know where he is or how to find him.'

'Did you know Deez is Mori's cousin?' said Chink.

'How the fuck do you know that,' Shorty responded, sitting forward.

'I know more than you might think. A number of Mori's little goons visit some of our fine establishments,' Chink responded, smirking. 'There's a few of them who are out every other night. Deez isn't one of them. He comes sometimes, but he's harder to get to.'

Marcus looked at the ground, scratching his chin, deep in thought. 'So who do you know?'

'As I said, there's a couple who are out a lot. Real party boys. One called Kyle, and one called Darryl. They won't get

AMBUSH

you close to Mori, but they can certainly get you closer to Deez.'

'So what's the play?' Marcus asked.

'Hang tight for now,' Chink said, Marcus deflating at his words. 'Don't worry, we will get them. But there's less risk in you two traipsing around town every night. I'm there anyway. If I see them in any of our spots, I'll let you know. Then you guys can do what you do best.' He looked from Marcus to Shorty.

Marcus smiled, stepping closer to Chink and touching fists with him. 'Good looking out, bro. You really came through for us.'

'Yeah, you have . . .' said Shorty, climbing to his feet and glaring at Chink. 'Why?'

Chink faced him down as if he had expected the resistance. 'Because it's the right thing to do. Mori is a problem, and problems need to be dealt with. Sometimes they cost you more than money,' he said, his eyes meeting Marcus's.

'So, you're going against your master? What do you think L will say about that?' Shorty continued.

Chink laughed. 'L keeps everyone in this room around him for one reason above all others; we do what we need to do when we need to do it. Sometimes that means stepping up rather than sitting around waiting for orders.'

'He's right,' Marcus agreed, laughing too, headache forgotten. Even Shorty cracked a smile.

'I feel you on that one,' said Shorty. 'I guess we'll hang tight then. You let us know when either of those dickheads surface.'

Chink nodded in response.

'Sorted. Chink will cover that angle. Shorty, link up with K-Bar and them lot. See what else you can dig up. I'm going to see how our friend Westy is getting on.' Marcus said with a sinister smile.

RICKY BLACK

Mori inhaled his spliff, exhaling the potent smoke, the air around him hazy as he considered his next move. Despite Wisdom's pledge of support, Mori had heard nothing from him, and didn't expect to. The more he considered his next steps, the more he realised how poorly organised the initial attack was. He'd assumed that the element of surprise would be enough to overcome Marcus, which, looking back, had been ridiculous. Mori hadn't even vetted the killers that Malston had hired.

Dumping the remains of the spliff into a nearby ashtray, he sat up, looking around the depressing spot he was holed up in. It was little more than a bedsit, with threadbare carpets, a mustard-coloured sofa that was stained in places, and an old television with only the basic channels. He didn't like to stay in a single spot for too long as a matter of principle, but he was already looking forward to the day he could leave this one. He wasn't particularly materialistic and didn't need much to keep him entertained, but the size of the place left him feeling cramped and claustrophobic.

Mori's frustration rose as the hours ticked on, and his team were often on the end of his outbursts.

Malston and Deez were solid and mostly dependable, but Mori had his fair share of *hangers-on*. The type of people who liked to be seen in the right circles, but didn't like getting their hands dirty. Mori knew Marcus's backing was different. Not only did Marcus have a team that rivalled Mori's, but Marcus's alliances also ran deep. With people like Shorty, K-Bar and Teflon waiting in the wings, Mori couldn't afford for his people to not be on point.

Mori closed his eyes, shaking his head. He needed more information to work with. He knew that Marcus also moved around a lot. He wouldn't be easy to get and would definitely be on guard. Mori hoped Wisdom could help, both with information and muscle. He was analytical, and useful in these sorts of situations.

When he was committed, anyway, Mori thought darkly. Mori's phone chirped, and he opened his eyes, scowling at the device. It made him miss the old days of pagers and phonebooks. Hearing the ring made him think of Marcus's threats, and, as Mori picked up the phone, he wondered who had given up his number.

'Yeah?' he answered.

'It's me,' said Malston. 'I ran into crackhead Nigel a bit ago. He had some shit to say.'

'Spit it out,' said Mori, in no mood for Malston's theatrics.

'He was begging money in Jukie's, and saw Tall-Man there.'

Mori instinctively straightened. Jukie's was neutral territory, but it still surprised him that Marcus would be out and about with everything going on.

'What was he doing?'

'He had a meeting with Lennox Thompson. Nige couldn't get close enough to hear what was said . . . Tall-Man would have probably ripped his head off if he tried. Anyway, he said they spoke, and then Marcus talked with another dude before he left.'

'And he didn't recognise the other dude? Was it Shorty?' Mori pressed, wondering who the man was.

'Nah, I think he'd know Shorty. He said the dude looked clean cut, but that he couldn't put a name to the face.'

Mori didn't speak. He didn't want to show it, but the revelation about Lennox had startled him. Lennox was formidable and feared in and around Leeds. Mori and Lennox had always been standoffish around each other. They weren't friends, but weren't enemies either. If he was standing with Marcus, it would make Mori's task all the more difficult.

'Mori?'

Mori shrugged off the ramifications. Ultimately, it

changed nothing. Whether Lennox got involved or not, Mori's task hadn't changed. He'd run through Lennox too if he got in his way.

'Don't worry about it, Malston. Have you spoken with any of the team?'

'Darryl. He was in a mood about something, though. Turns out—'

'I don't give a shit,' Mori snapped, uninterested in their personal lives. 'Tell them to pull their fingers out and get sorted. We're at fucking war,' he said.

'I know, Mori. We'll sort it. Don't worry.'

'I'll speak to you later.' Mori hung up, scowling into space.

CHAPTER SEVEN

THE NEXT NIGHT, Marcus sat in the safe house. He'd yet to go out, instead spending most of his time indoors, making phone calls and working out. He felt a little better after his conversations with Lennox, Shorty and Chink. It was nice to have support in the moves he wanted to make. He wished Lamont was on board with him, but was trying not to over-think it.

Sheldon's words about the police weighed on his mind. He wasn't shocked they'd connected the deaths in Little London to him, but they lacked proof and motive, which was likely why he hadn't heard anything official. He would still need to take care when making moves, but it was a positive. The last thing he needed was to give them an excuse to focus on him.

Grabbing his phone, he called Georgia, wanting to speak with her before he went to see Westy.

'Hey, Georgia,' he said, when she answered.

'Hi.'

An awkward silence ensued. Marcus tried again.

'How are you doing?'

'Fine.'

Marcus shook his head.

'G, I'm working on it. Like I told you, once it's sorted, everything goes back to normal. Is your sis alright?'

'She's fine, Marcus. Both of us are. Is there anything else you wanted?'

'I wanted to check on you, obviously. I know you're pissed, but this is for your own good. Do you need anything?'

'No. I'm fine,' said Georgia.

'Cool. I'm gonna send you money, anyway. As soon as I can.'

'Okay. Guess I'll speak to you later,' said Georgia.

'G . . . I love you,' Marcus said. There was another pause.

'I love you too.'

Marcus hung up, tempted to go and see her. He didn't like hearing her sounding so distant on the phone, but it couldn't be helped right now. Going to see her would be too risky, and he knew it.

Considering who he could use to send her money, Marcus settled on Chink. He was unthreatening, and would make a good go-between for Marcus and Georgia. Resolving to speak to Chink about it at a later date, he left his safe house, and drove to Westy's. Exiting the car with a spring in his step, he swung the door closed. Their plan was in motion, and he was keen to get things moving.

Having parked down the road, he approached on foot. Arriving at Westy's door, he rapped on it rhythmically, stepping back when the door swung open.

Westy's grin faltered when he saw Marcus, the colour draining from his face.

'I come in peace,' said Marcus, holding his hands up and smiling. The words didn't appear to reassure Westy. He shifted awkwardly, hanging onto the door frame.'Westy, are you not gonna invite me in? We're friends.'

Saying nothing, Westy stepped to the side, allowing Marcus to enter.

AMBUSH

'Where's your woman?' said Marcus, looking around the house before plopping himself on the sofa. He pulled the gun out of the waistband of his bottoms, resting it on his lap. Marcus's mouth twitched as he saw Westy's eyes flit from the gun to Marcus, his eyes wide. 'Chill. It just wasn't comfortable there.'

Westy shifted awkwardly again, his eyes still fixed on the gun.

'She's staying with a friend. Didn't want her around. Just in case.'

'Smart,' Marcus said, pushing his bottom lip above the top one and nodding. His mind flitted back to Georgia. Her hostility towards him was frustrating. Marcus didn't want to uproot and inconvenience her, but it was his only choice. He hoped she would see sense soon enough. Marcus had people watching her sister's house, but it didn't stop him worrying.

'Erm … what can I help you with,' said Westy, breaking Marcus's quiet reflection.

Blinking, Marcus took a moment before focusing on Westy.

'How are you feeling?' he said.

Westy looked confused.

'I'm alright, I suppose . . .'

'I don't mean generally. After the beating. Are you all healed up?' Marcus asked, watching Westy hesitate.

'I … guess so,' Westy responded.

'Good. I didn't want to hurt you too badly. Especially when you started cooperating. Now, if you hadn't . . . that would have been a whole other story.' Marcus picked the gun up, turning it in his hands and staring down at it. After a moment, he placed it back on his lap. 'You're going to cooperate the same way now, aren't you?'

Westy nodded.

'Good. So, tell me more about Mori. What do you know about the setup?'

'Nothing. He told me about the job and to lure you there. Said you trusted me; that his shooting team would take you out. He said there would be no retaliation.'

'When did he approach you?'

'Two weeks ago.'

'Why didn't you tell me? You had two weeks where you could have let me know.' Marcus appeared calm, but his eyes were blazing. He felt the anger raging inside of him, struggling to control it. There was nothing stopping him from ending Westy here and now. The house was empty. There were no witnesses. He caressed the frame of the gun with his forefinger. Westy's response would determine his fate.

'Well?'

Westy was sweating, his lips trembling with terror as he shook his head.

'Mori had people watching me, bro. He threatened to rape Chelsea and cut her tongue out in front of me.'

'You think I wouldn't do that?' Marcus asked softly. 'The cutting, anyway. I'm not a rapist.'

'I know you would, but I didn't have a choice,' said Westy, sighing. He'd finally stopped shaking, but looked increasingly uncomfortable.

'So, if I told you to take this gun and go to Mori's place and cap him, what would you say?' Marcus asked.

'I'd s-say that I don't know where he lives, and that he will definitely be on the move. Everyone knows the hit failed. Mori will have gone to ground if he's smart.'

'Mori didn't say anything about taking on the job for anyone? He didn't say anything about the people he was working with?'

'No. Why would he tell me that?'

'Because he's a little prick who likes to show off and pretend he's clever. I think it's exactly the kind of thing he would do,' said Marcus.

AMBUSH

Westy shifted in his seat, his eyes darting from side to side. He was holding something back, Marcus was sure of it.

'Well, he didn't,' said Westy, clasping his hands together and glancing at the ground.

In one smooth motion, Marcus snatched up his gun and aimed it at Westy's chest.

'Do you think I'm fucking playing? I've tried to be nice and give you a chance to tell me what's going on. If you're no use to me . . .'

'Alright! Alright! I'll tell you. Just please, put that thing down,' Westy replied, throwing his hands up in the air in surrender.

Marcus smirked, placing the gun on the coffee table, sliding to his feet and towering over the terrified man.

'Go on then. Tell me everything. And I mean *everything*.'

'Mori was saying you had a lot of enemies in different camps, and I would be doing a lot of powerful people a favour if I worked against you.'

Marcus mulled it over for a moment. 'So he *is* working with people,' he concluded.

'I don't know, I swear. That's all he said. I really am sorry, Marcus. He didn't give me a choice.'

Marcus continued to look off into space, pondering what this could mean. After a moment, he turned back to Westy.

'You fucked up, Westy. You could have told me. We'd have sorted it and you'd have been protected. I hope you know that. You're on your own now. Whoever he's got working with him will soon find out who they're dealing with.'

Marcus looked at Westy a moment longer, the fear visible in his eyes. Walking backwards a couple of paces, he turned to face the door, and exited onto the street.

CHAPTER EIGHT

THE NEXT DAY, Marcus was sat indoors, half-asleep, with an *X-Raided* CD playing in the background. When his phone rang, he grumbled to himself and picked it up, eyebrows raising when he saw Lamont's name.

'What's happening?' he asked.

'How's everything going?' Lamont replied. Marcus rolled his eyes. It was typical of Lamont to answer a question with another question.

'Everything's fine. You checking up on me or something?'

'Would it be such a bad thing if I was?'

'For fuck's sake, L. Do you ever answer a question?'

Lamont chuckled. 'Sorry, force of habit. I guess you could consider this a check-in. I have news too, but that doesn't mean I don't worry about you.'

'I told you before, L. I'm the last person you need to worry about. Everything's cool over here. What's the news?'

'I've set up a meeting with Wisdom.'

'Why?' Marcus frowned at the phone.

'I don't want to get into too much over the phone. Can we link up later in the evening? Let me know where you'll be about five, six o'clock, and I'll fly over.'

AMBUSH

'That'll work. Catch you then.' Marcus hung up, wondering about the call. It was good that Lamont was showing out for him, but Marcus was sceptical of anything that Wisdom would have to say, especially concerning Mori. Sliding to his feet, he turned up the music and started cranking out press-ups.

THAT EVENING, Lamont stood in the middle of the room. He was dressed for the winter weather in a fleece jacket, a sweater underneath, and jogging bottoms. The gloves he'd worn when he entered were on the coffee table, alongside a Paul & Shark woolly hat.

'What's going on then? What does Wisdom have for us?' Marcus asked, still slumped on the sofa. He'd let Lamont in, then retook his seat.

'He may have nothing,' said Lamont. 'I thought a face-to-face with him would be a good avenue to pursue, and we can take it from there.'

'Wisdom is full of shit,' said Marcus. 'I don't have the same level of trust for him that you do.'

'I know that, and that's why I'll be there to ensure things run smoothly. You don't have to go. I'm in no way insisting on it, but I thought it might help.'

Marcus mulled it over. He appreciated the fact Lamont was leaving the decision up to him, rather than telling him what to do.

'Are we meeting on his turf?'

'I didn't think you'd want him knowing where you were staying.' Lamont glanced around the cramped room. 'I doubt there would be enough space for us to have a meeting here, anyway.'

Marcus sniggered.

'Fine. I'll go. I'm not promising that dickhead anything,

though, but I'll hear him out.'

'That's all I ask for. I appreciate you trusting me on this.'

'You're my brother, L,' said Marcus. 'If I can't trust you, I can't trust anyone.'

It was the truth. Marcus had known Lamont since they were kids. They had lived together when Lamont's Auntie adopted Marcus and, after a rough start, they'd become close, always looking out for one another. Marcus didn't want anything to come between that.

Lamont smiled, patting Marcus on the shoulder.

'Come, let's slide. I need to stop somewhere, so I'll drive us.'

Marcus grabbed a jacket and gloves, heading out to Lamont's car. He had his gun in his jacket pocket, just in case he needed it.

'Watch the bag when you're getting in,' said Lamont. Marcus looked down, seeing a *One2One* bag on the passenger seat.

'What's in there?' he asked, placing it on his lap as Lamont started the engine.

'Marika needed a new phone.'

Marcus chuckled. 'I thought you gave her money for one before?'

Lamont drove away from the safe house, grinning.

'I did.'

The pair both shared a laugh, aware of Lamont's little sister and her ways. Their parents had died when they were young, and he'd looked out for his sister where possible ever since. They were close, and by extension, Marcus too, saw her as a little sister. She was two years younger, and had been spoiled all her life. Lamont and Marcus had always struggled to say no to her and, when they did, she had an incredible knack for finding what she wanted elsewhere.

They drove to Marika's place, a flat near Harehills Avenue. Parking up, they climbed from the car, Marcus handing the bag to Lamont. When they were let into the complex, they took the stairs to her flat on the first floor, Lamont walking straight in.

'Rika, you need to be locking your door,' he said. 'Anyone could walk in.'

'I knew you were coming,' a voice loudly called out. Marcus and Lamont entered the living room. The light was on, along with two candles on the mantlepiece. The room was cramped, but cosy, with a corner sofa taking up a significant proportion of the room. The television and DVD player were both top-of-the-line, and the carpets were plush, a light blue decor giving the room a calming vibe.

On the sofa, Marika sat, along with several friends. She wore one of Lamont's old Nike sweaters with leggings and a pair of fluffy slippers. She grinned at Lamont, then gave Marcus a fond smile.

'Regardless, you need to take security more seriously,' Lamont said.

Marika rolled her eyes.

'You two are the scariest things likely to ever walk through that door,' she said, looking the pair up and down, smiling.

She moved to get up, but Lamont held out his hand.

'You don't need to move, sis.' He headed over, giving her a hug and a kiss, Marcus doing the same. They greeted Marika's friends, then focused on her.

Marcus had known Marika since she was a little girl, and as she'd grown up, she'd developed stunning good looks. She was taller than her friends, had long dark hair, blemish-free skin and eyes similar to Lamont's. Since hitting her teens, she had been a problem, and both Marcus and Lamont had warned several men away from her.

Despite their efforts, she was three months pregnant, and beginning to show.

'Here,' said Lamont, handing her the bag. She opened it,

squealing when she saw the Nokia 8310, flashing it to her friends. They grinned at her, but didn't speak. Marcus noticed that they would act nervous whenever Lamont was around. He often watched as their eyes flicked to Lamont, to each other, and then down to the ground. They were like little girls in the playground, staring at the popular guy three years above them. Marcus found it amusing, particularly considering the issues Lamont had when he was in school.

Marcus's eyes traced from Marika's friends to the table. There was a bottle of brandy sitting there, along with a two-litre bottle of Lilt, and several glasses. Marcus lifted his head, looking from the table to Lamont, who caught his eye.

'I hope you're not drinking while you're pregnant?' Lamont said, shooting her two friends a dark look, the pair quailing under the gaze. Marika rolled her eyes, unaffected.

'I'm being good, L. Promise. I'm just drinking the Lilt. Check my glass if you don't believe me.'

Marika extended her arm, wafting the glass in the air in front of Lamont's face.

'I believe you, sis. Chill. I'm just checking.' Lamont gave her another hug before stepping away. 'We need to go somewhere, but ring me if you need anything, and I'll check in on you later.'

'Thanks, bro. Love you.'

After saying their goodbyes, Lamont and Marcus left. When they were back in the car, Marcus elbowed his friend.

'You're a soft bastard, you know that, don't you?'

'Whatever, Marcus. I saw the money you slipped her when we were leaving. You're as soft as I am.'

Laughing, they drove to Wisdom's, enjoying the moment of levity.

———

AMBUSH

MARCUS AND LAMONT entered the dark, dank room, sharing a look before taking their seats. In the middle of the room stood an old wooden table; chipped and slashed in various places, a bottle of vodka and three small glasses sitting in the centre of it. The seats, which looked like they'd come as a set, creaked as the pair dropped their weight onto them.

Marcus struggled to adjust to the low light. A single light bulb hovered above the table, casting a glow across their faces, but leaving much of the room in darkness.

Lamont sat silent, eyes fixed on the door they were both facing. Marcus shot sideways glances at his friend for a short while, before stretching out, picking up one of the glasses and adding a generous helping of vodka to it. After draining the glass in one motion, he refilled his glass and placed it in front of him on the table.

'Where the fuck is he?' Marcus asked, glaring at the door.

'You know Wisdom,' Lamont replied. 'He has a flair for the dramatic.'

Marcus smirked in response, tapping his long thin fingers on the table.

A few moments later, the door creaked as it swung open. Wisdom made his way into the room, followed by a skinny thug Marcus knew as *Sonny Black*. Wordlessly, Wisdom directed Sonny to stand in the corner. Standing behind the only empty chair for a moment, Wisdom looked from Lamont to Marcus, his face unreadable.

'Gentlemen,' he said, as he scraped the chair along the floor, repositioning it and taking his seat.

'Thanks for agreeing to meet with us, Wisdom,' Lamont responded.

'I was as keen as you to get around the table, L. This shit that's gone on . . . it's madness.'

Lamont nodded. 'Hopefully, we can all agree on a way forward that's mutually beneficial.'

Marcus's stare burned into the side of Lamont's head, but

his friend was unmoved. It was no surprise to see Lamont so calm, but to see him setting the foundations for peaceful negotiations irked Marcus. He had been attacked and almost killed, but his friend was more concerned with business. He was placing more stock in the weight of his wallet than the weight of their friendship.

Slowly pulling his eyes away from Lamont, Marcus looked across the table, seeing Wisdom eyeing him with curiosity.

'What the fuck are you looking at?'

Wisdom's eyebrows shot up. Lamont turned sharply, looking across at his friend. Marcus didn't move, content to stare Wisdom down.

'I'm sure you can understand Marcus's outburst, Wisdom,' Lamont started hurriedly. 'What happened shouldn't have. I'm sure between us we can get to the bottom of it. Is there anything you can tell us?'

Wisdom continued to look at Marcus for a moment before fixing his eyes on Lamont. 'Mori didn't speak to me about any of it. Had he spoken to me, I'd have told him Marcus was off limits. Mori is wild, but he's loyal. It was an error in judgement, but not one that had any major consequences.'

Marcus's mind flashed back to the spot he had been duped into raiding. He blinked as the faces of the kids he had taken with him flitted into his mind and out.

'*No major consequences*? Three kids were killed,' Marcus said, leaning forward and resting his elbows on the table.

Wisdom nodded.

'If we were talking about you losing your regulars, that would be another matter. But we're not.' Wisdom left it hanging in the air for a moment.

Lamont shot a glance across at his friend. Looking down at his glass, Marcus downed his drink. Picking up the bottle, he poured another generous measurement.

'I don't give a fuck if they weren't my regulars. They were

kids, Wisdom. They deserved better.'

'They knew the risk when —'

'Don't talk to me about fucking risk!' roared Marcus, his fist crashing down on the table, causing the two unused glasses to topple over. 'Your boy brought the risk setting us up. It was a routine snatch. Something I've done a thousand times. Why do you think I took them?' he demanded, veins pulsating in his temples.

Wisdom's eyes widened. Sonny took a step out of his corner.

Surveying the room, Lamont waited a beat before speaking.

'Tempers are high. They were always going to be, but I have to believe there's common ground to be had here.'

Marcus said nothing.

'Agreed,' Wisdom responded, turning his attention to Lamont.

'So you say Mori went rogue on this one. He works for you. Doesn't he check in and tell you what he's planning?' Lamont asked.

'Marcus works for you,' Wisdom replied, motioning to him with his thumb. 'Does he tell you everything he gets up to?'

'Marcus doesn't work for me. He works *with me* occasionally, but he does his own thing. I don't interrupt. I'm here as his friend, not his boss. You said it yourself; what's happened is madness. We need to sort it. Nobody wants a war, Wisdom. You more so than most.' Lamont let the statement hang for a moment.

Marcus looked at Lamont out of the corner of his eye. His face had changed. It was harder now. There was a shift in his approach, and, although subtle, the true meaning of what Lamont had said was clear.

Wisdom scratched his chin for a moment, looking past Lamont and Marcus.

'I agree, L . . . but I can't control Mori.' He said, shoulders slumping.

'Can you get hold of him, at least? See if he's open to a meeting.'

Before Wisdom could answer, Marcus flared up once more.

'Wait a fucking minute,' he said. 'I'm not agreeing to meet with Mori to be set up. It's not going down like that.'

'Wisdom would, I'm sure, ensure Mori and his people are aware of the rules of engagement.' Lamont inclined his eyebrows to Wisdom, directing him to take over.

'It's true,' he said. 'I would have. Unfortunately, I'm not sure I can get in touch with him. I have a number for him, but he barely answers it. He comes around every now and again. I can get a message to him, but I don't know when that will be. If your people can hang fire while I hear back from him, I'm sure we can arrange something.'

Marcus's eyes narrowed. It was difficult to understand how Wisdom wouldn't have a direct line of communication with Mori, given their relationship. It appeared Wisdom was trying to buy time; giving Mori a window to fortify and strategise.

Marcus didn't like it.

Picking his drink up once more and draining it, he slid the chair out from underneath him and rose to his feet.

'It's in your interests to find him, Wisdom.'

Wisdom's demeanour slipped as he glanced up at Marcus.

'Are you threatening me?' he said.

Over Wisdom's shoulder, Marcus noted Sonny moving ever closer. 'I've played ball. I came here tonight at L's request. I told him it would come to nothing, but I came because he asked me. I'll be damned if I'm sitting on my arse while Mori plots away in the background with the time you've bought him. You fucking find him and give him up, or you go too.'

AMBUSH

'Marcus –'

'No, L. This guy isn't gonna help us. Mori is his boy. For all we know, this little fucking snake ordered the hit,' Marcus said, fury burning in his dark eyes.

Wisdom sat in place dumbstruck, still looking up at Marcus.

'You come into my spot . . . disrespecting me. Threatening me. Who the fuck do you think you are?' he said incredulously.

'You know exactly who I am,' Marcus replied. 'And if you don't give up what you know, I'll be your worst fucking nightmare.'

Marcus placed his hands on the table, leaning closer to Wisdom as he spoke. After a moment, he straightened up, taking two steps back.

'You've got a day, Wisdom. Get what you know to L. After that, there's a green light on Mori and everybody who rolls with him.' Marcus swung the door open sharply, the force sending it careering into the wall. Without looking back, he left the room.

Lamont and Wisdom stared at each other for a moment. Rising to his feet, Lamont tucked his chair neatly beneath the damaged table, and nodded to Wisdom, a resigned expression on his face.

'I'll be in touch,' Lamont said. 'Let me know if you dig anything up.'

Wisdom didn't speak, content to return his nod of understanding. His eyes followed Lamont as he made his way to the door.

Taking a brief moment to survey any damage Marcus might have caused, Lamont returned to the table and dropped a stack of notes onto it.

'For the wall,' he said, turning immediately and following Marcus's lead.

RICKY BLACK

———

Neither Marcus nor Lamont spoke as they drove from the meeting. Lamont had his eyes on the road, his expression natural. Marcus, on the other hand, couldn't relax. Wisdom had tried to play him for a fool, and the more he thought about it, the angrier he got. He didn't trust Wisdom, and never had. The fact he'd slithered out of taking responsibility for Mori or providing any real support was telling, and he was glad he'd reacted as he had.

Marcus's only regret was that he hadn't damaged Wisdom and his lackey, as well as his wall.

'Well, that could have gone better,' said Lamont, sarcasm oozing from him.

'Did you see Sonny trying to creep up on me? Skinny little prick,' Marcus growled. 'I'd rip his spine out if he ever stepped to me.'

Lamont shook his head, indicating, then taking a left turn.

'I wish you would understand that showing emotion around people you don't trust just makes you look weak.'

'You better watch your mouth, calling me weak,' Marcus warned Lamont.

'Fine. Can't you see that working this way only makes our jobs harder?' Lamont continued. 'Not only that, it gives Wisdom more reason to work against us.'

'I made the decision to take the youths on the job,' said Marcus. 'I've gotta live with that. I can deal with that.' Marcus pointed a shaky finger at Lamont, still furious. 'What I won't deal with is that snake not giving a shit. He didn't care that they got killed. He wasn't interested in helping either. He was buying his boy time. That's it.'

'All the more reason not to alienate him, Marcus,' said Lamont. 'I'm not saying he's right, and I'm certainly not saying I agree, but sometimes you have to conceal what you're thinking, because it throws everyone else off. If they

AMBUSH

can't prepare for you, then they can't prepare. It's a mental battle, as well as business, that's all I'm saying.'

Marcus simply grunted, not wanting to have the conversation. Marcus saw no reason to pussyfoot around people like Wisdom. He wasn't a threat, and if he impeded Marcus in any way, he would deal with him, Mori, and Sonny Black too.

Giving Marcus one last glance, Lamont realised his words hadn't been taken on board, consigning himself to the silence that engulfed them.

———

MORI SAT in the same dark room that Lamont and Marcus had vacated just hours earlier. Slouching in his chair, he rapped his fingers on the table, paying little attention to Wisdom.

'Are you listening to me, Mori?' Wisdom said, eyes bulging.

'Yeah,' Mori replied, not meeting Wisdom's eyes.

'I'm having trouble believing that. When I'm talking to you, you're not responding or reacting. You're just sat there tip-tapping your fucking fingers on the table like a school kid.'

'What do you want me to say?' Mori replied, looking up at Wisdom with a broad smile on his face.

'I want you to tell me you had a plan all along. That you know how to get us out of this stuff you've caused. That you can get at Daniels and that you've not left us up a creek and in the shit!'

Mori continued to look into Wisdom's eyes, the smug smirk ever widening. After a moment, he merely shrugged, returning to the table and tapping it some more.

'And what the fuck is that supposed to mean?' Wisdom said incredulously, imitating the motion.

Finally, Mori's smile vanished. 'Are you taking the piss out of me?' he said, leaning closer to Wisdom.

'Oh, you're going to start with me now?' Wisdom said, eyebrows raised in mock confusion. 'Because obviously Marcus . . . and Teflon . . . and Shorty . . . and Lennox aren't enough for you.' Wisdom counted on his fingers as he recited the names of the people Mori had aligned against. 'Please let me know if I've missed anyone, but I'm afraid I'm running out of fingers.'

'Lennox won't roll with Marcus,' Mori said, looking down at the ground.

'Oh, great. Best adjust these then,' said Wisdom, pushing down one of his fingers. 'Just Marcus, Lamont and Shorty then. Tons better,' he concluded.

'Say what you like. There's no going back now. You're with me or you're against me. It's that simple. Choose.'

The pair's eyes met as the statement hung in the air. Mori turned his head slightly as he analysed his long-term partner.

'He was here earlier, you know.' Wisdom finally answered.

'Who was?' Mori asked, somehow already knowing the answer.

'Marcus. Sitting right there in that chair.' Wisdom motioned with his hand. Mori's top lip curled like a terrible smell had invaded his nostrils. 'Do you know what he said to me?' Mori shook his head. 'He told me if I don't give you up, I'm in his crosshairs too.'

Mori's eyes narrowed, watching as Wisdom sat back in his chair.

Was this it? Was Wisdom really going to give him up?

'So, what now?' He asked, sitting up and steeling himself. Wisdom waited a beat before responding.

'We get him first,' he said. 'You know where my loyalty lies. If it wasn't sealed before he came to see me, his fate was by the time he left.'

A wicked grin stretched Mori's cheeks.

'Let me know what you need. You have my backing.

AMBUSH

People, tools, whatever. Just shout up, and it's yours. I'll try to play both sides from a distance. See what I can dig up that might help you,' Wisdom finished.

Again, Mori's eyes narrowed. 'You wouldn't be trying to hedge your bets now, would you?'

'Think what you want, Mori. Nobody speaks to me how Marcus did. Bear that in mind. The support I've offered can easily be taken away.'

Mori scratched his chin as he considered Wisdom's words. After a moment, he nodded.

'What about Teflon?' He leaned forward once more, clasping his hands together.

Looking up into the air, Wisdom rubbed his wrist.

'I'll see how long I can convince him I'm neutral for. If he cottons onto what I'm doing, he will need to go too.'

Licking his lips, Mori grinned.

'Do you think we have the people to take him out?'

'I'm not sure. A lot of what happens now is in fate's hands. If he knows I'm all in, he will be too. If we can keep it you vs Marcus for a while, it might keep him away from direct involvement. I think that's our best shot for now.'

After a moment, Mori nodded.

'I have to say, I didn't think you would have the stones for this,' he said, smiling across at Wisdom.

A dark look descended on his partner's face. 'Make no mistake about my intentions,' he said. 'I wish I wasn't having to make these decisions. We were doing fine. You got us caught up in this shit, and I'm having to help clean up the mess.'

Smirking, Mori rose to his feet. 'There's the Wisdom I know and love,' he said, making his way to the door. 'Thanks for the support.'

Swinging the door closed behind him before Wisdom could respond, he left.

CHAPTER NINE

MARCUS SAT in one of the crew's better spots, surrounded by his closest confidants. The spot was well furnished, with a three-seater sofa, armchair, coffee table, and a plush carpet that seemed overly luxurious for the property. A television sat in front of the sofa with a games console hooked up to it. Sitting on a chest of drawers, a sound system pumped music into the room.

K-Bar and Shorty bumped their heads along to the music, glancing every now and again at Marcus. Sitting on the edge of the sofa, his eyes were fixed on the mobile phone laying on the coffee table.

Shorty stood, heading over to the sound system and turning the music down. Plopping himself down beside Marcus, he glanced from the phone to his friend.

'They're not gonna call, Marcus. You know that.'

Marcus stared at the phone for a moment longer before glancing at Shorty. 'I know,' he responded. 'They've got five more minutes. I gave Wisdom twenty-four hours. I'm a man of my word.'

'Well, can we turn this shit back up then?' K-Bar asked, smiling. 'I was just getting into it.'

AMBUSH

'Listen to it later,' said Shorty.

Shrugging, K-Bar didn't bother arguing the point. Minutes later, both men straightened when they saw Marcus rise to his feet. Extending his wrist and checking his watch, Marcus's eyes flitted from his watch, to his phone, and back again.

'Time's up,' he said. Snatching up his phone, he faced Shorty and K-Bar. 'K, you know what to do. I want you and your guys out scouring the streets for anybody associated with Mori. There's a green light on anybody you find. Do what you do best.'

K-Bar nodded in response. Shorty straightened as Marcus focused his attention on him.

'Shorty, team up with Blakey. We know Mori's guys like a night out. See if we can catch them slipping.'

Shorty rubbed his hands together as a smile spread across his face.

'Leave it with me, fam. I was thirsty anyway.' He licked his lips.

'Stay focused. We can't have you fucking around and getting caught out,' said Marcus, eyes narrowed.

Shorty's face immediately dropped.

'I can handle my fucking business,' he said, frowning at his friend. Marcus nodded, rubbing his forehead and closing his eyes for a moment.

'I know, bro. Sorry. The stakes are high on this one. I just wanna make sure everybody's on point.'

Shorty nodded.

'We've got you, bro. Don't worry about a thing.'

———

SHELDON STOOD in front of the house on Oatland Close. Blue and white tape fluttered in the winter wind whipping through Little London. Zipping his coat up to the top, Sheldon turned on the spot and set off across the road.

His eyes flitted left to right as he moved. Climbing onto the curb, he stopped for a moment, pulling out his notebook and pencil. Observing the book, he reviewed the houses he'd already visited. Pointing to the houses with his pencil, he mouthed the numbers as his hand moved across them.

'32,' he said, circling the number in the notepad and then placing it in his pocket.

Sheldon stepped through the gate, carefully setting it back in place. Walking to the door, he knocked and stepped back. After a moment, the door opened a crack. Two big brown eyes stared out at him, magnified comically by a pair of thick glasses resting on a concerned-looking face.

'Can I help you?'

'I hope so,' Sheldon replied, smiling.

The woman's eyes flitted between the officer and the house across the street.

'If it's about what happened across the way, I didn't see anything,' she said.

Sheldon stepped forward, placing his foot on the bottom step.

'I know it's tough to remember when something as horrible as this happens, but in these situations, we often find the right questions help to prompt people's memory. If I can just come inside for a —'

'I'm sorry. I really can't help you. I didn't see anything,' the woman interrupted, slamming the door.

Sheldon stood for a moment, observing the spot where the magnified eyes had vacated. Blowing out a breath, he took out his notepad and struck through number 32.

Making his way back across the street, he lifted the blue and white tape, stepping into the garden.

'No luck,' Sheldon said, addressing his colleague.

'I could tell,' the officer responded. 'Heard the door slam from over here.'

Sheldon looked the grey-bricked house up and down,

analysing the situation. It contained all the evidence they needed to establish what had happened, but not enough to provide them with a suitable suspect. They badly needed witnesses, but their search had been fruitless. Even the victims' families had been uncooperative.

It didn't surprise Sheldon. It followed a well-established pattern. He assumed the families' silence had been bought; one way or another. It left little hope of finding the culprit, and frustrations running high. Sheldon had his suspicions, but law and order dealt with facts, not hunches.

'I tell you what, if her across the street didn't see what happened, we've got no chance,' the officer continued.

Sheldon pulled his gaze from the house, looking at his colleague, confused.

'Did you see the size of them jam jars on her head?' he asked, a wide grin on his face. Sheldon snorted.

'I don't think not being able to see is their issue,' he said, focusing on the house again. 'They're scared to talk.'

The officer nodded.

'There's only a few people around here I can think of that could instill that kind of fear in a person.'

'I was thinking the same.'

'You still like Daniels for this?' the officer said, motioning to the house. Sheldon shrugged.

'It makes sense, right? The kids are known to have been affiliated with him – however loosely. Our intel tells us the shooters had a solid reputation for being skilled and dependable. One person walked away with their life, that much the evidence tells us. We've got people in the street scared shitless, trying to convince us they didn't hear guns blasting off. It feels beyond coincidental,' Sheldon concluded.

'But we don't have the evidence to convict?'

'But we don't have the evidence to convict,' Sheldon repeated.

The officer looked from Sheldon to the house, shaking his head.

'So what now?' he asked. Sheldon turned on the spot, focusing on his colleague.

'We keep going,' he said. 'We keep working until we find that key piece of evidence that cracks the case wide open. We turn whispers and rumours into facts and statements. We get our guy, whether that's Daniels or some other scumbag.'

Nodding to the officer, Sheldon moved to the crime tape, lifting it up and stepping under it. Making his way across the road, he took his notepad back out, circling *number 34* and stepping through the gate.

CHAPTER TEN

SHORTY WAS in the club with Blakey, hanging back and watching the people around him. He held a warm bottle of beer that he'd been nursing since they entered. They'd been in the club for an hour, but nothing stood out.

Shorty and Blakey had mostly kept to themselves, dancing with a few girls, but generally keeping a low profile. It was a complicated operation. Shorty wanted to be close to the action, so he had the best possible vantage point, but he didn't want to be seen by the wrong people.

Draining his drink, he nodded to Blakey, signalling for him to go to the bar.

Shorty took a moment to observe a group of women standing near him. When he was confident none of them knew Stacey, he moved forward, introducing himself. They were the perfect cover, he mused. They were mostly plain and unassuming, and Shorty was sure few eyes would be drawn their way.

'Blakey, these are my new friends,' Shorty shouted over the music. Blakey smirked as he observed the woman standing closest to Shorty eying him hungrily.

'Nice to meet you all,' Blakey said, holding out his hand.

Shorty looked down at his friend's hand before meeting his eyes. Pushing his hand away, the girls stepped forward, introducing themselves and each hugging Blakey in turn.

'You've got no fucking game,' Shorty said out of the side of his mouth when the mob had dispersed.

'What do you mean?' Blakey responded, nonplussed.

'I mean holding out your fucking hand like you're at a job interview,' said Shorty laughing. 'Don't worry, I'll teach you someday.' Shorty thumped Blakey on the back, sending a jolt through his body.

'Thanks,' Blakey replied, scrunching up his face and rubbing his back.

'Looks like it's a no-go in here, anyway. Wanna try somewhere else? Chink told me some kid called Kyle never misses a Thursday night,' Shorty said.

'Why Thursday night?' Blakey enquired, looking confused.

'Look around you,' said Shorty smiling. 'Student night.'

Blakey looked around the club, his eyes widening.

'Fucking hell, they all look about twelve.'

'We've been here two hours now, Blakey. If you hadn't noticed before now, I think I need a new scouting partner,' Shorty chuckled to himself. 'Come on. Let's bounce. See if we have any luck over the road.'

———

While Shorty and Blakey were in town, Marcus, K-Bar and Sharma prowled around the Hood, searching for signs of Mori and his people. They had seen nothing, but were determined not to give up.

'Keep the speed level, Sharma. We don't want to get pulled over.'

'I know, Tall-Man. I know what I'm doing, bro.'

Marcus didn't reply. He eyed K-Bar, looking out of the

window, completely at peace. Marcus had always admired that about K-Bar. It took a lot to shock him, and he was always down for the cause and willing to help. Marcus respected those traits.

'You heard from Shorty?' he asked. K-Bar nodded.

'He hasn't found anything yet. Him and Blakey are in town. They thought they would be able to find Kyle, but it looks like he's laying low.'

'Kyle's a fucking loser, anyway, if it's the one I'm thinking of. Doubt he would be able to help us if we found him.'

'Would give us a start, I guess. Would be better than what we've got now,' K-Bar responded, still staring off airily into the distance.

'I suppose so,' Marcus said, turning to look out of his own window as Sharma drove on in silence.

———

SHORTY AND BLAKEY quickly regretted their decision to switch bars. There was less room to manoeuvre, and more faces that Shorty recognised. Keeping a low profile had become increasingly more challenging.

They were sipping brandy and cokes near the bar when Blakey suddenly got Shorty's attention.

'That dude over there. The one in the black jacket and red t-shirt.'

Shorty covertly glanced in the direction Blakey had hinted at, looking at the guy in question. He was tall and broad-shouldered, with cornrowed hair. Shorty's eyes narrowed as he finally placed the man.

'Is that Darryl?'

Blakey nodded.

'Yeah. He's a nobody, but he chills with Kyle and some of Mori's other guys. Matches the pics Chink gave us of his people. How do you wanna play it?'

Shorty was already moving, making his way through the crowd. Before Darryl realised what was going on, Shorty was in his space, his hand resting on the man's shoulder.

'Yes, Darryl, what you saying, man?'

Darryl's face paled. He tried to turn, but Shorty increased the pressure on his shoulder, making the man wince.

'Don't treat me like an idiot. Stay where you are, and I'll buy you a drink.'

Shorty signalled to the barmaid, who hurried to the fridge, pulled out a bottle of beer and handed it across the bar. Grabbing it with his free hand, Shorty pushed it toward Darryl.

Darryl's eyes traced down his top, looking at the beer that had sloshed down his front. Meeting Shorty's eyes briefly, he looked left and right, his eyes widening as a gap appeared in the crowd.

As he motioned to move, Blakey stepped into his path, cutting off his escape route.

'What's happening, Shorty? How are you doing?' Darryl asked, resigned to his fate.

Shorty shrugged. 'You know me. My team is on top of the world, and we're all making money. How's your team doing?'

'I don't have a team,' replied Darryl, looking around again. Shorty smiled.

'Relax. I know you're cool with Mori, and that's alright. We don't need to get involved in the war yet. I just wanna talk. Why don't we get out of here, go somewhere and talk about our people, and then come back?' Shorty pulled a few notes out of his pocket, seeing Darryl's eyes gleam when he saw the money. 'You might make yourself a bit of change out of it.'

Darryl mulled it over for a moment and then nodded.

It was packed outside, the streets and roads lined with people spilling out of various neon-lighted bars and clubs. Shorty surveyed the scene for a moment, as Blakey pulled out his phone and made a call.

AMBUSH

Darryl stood awkwardly, looking from Shorty to Blakey.

'Yeah, come and pick us up. Bottom of town, yeah.' Blakey hung up, turning to face Shorty. 'We're on,' he said.

Shorty didn't respond for a moment. His head tilted as he watched a middle-aged man attempt to guide a drunk student into a taxi. Shorty turned to Darryl and smiled.

'Chill out. We'll take care of you. I promise you, you're safer with us than she is with him,' Shorty said, motioning to the taxi now driving away.

Twenty minutes later, they were in a car being driven out of town. They stopped at a house in Chapeltown, and Shorty led the group in, locking the door behind them.

Darryl was told to take a seat. Shorty remained standing, nodding at Blakey, who promptly left the room. He assessed Darryl, watching him grow more nervous under pressure. Finally, he stepped forward, grinning when he saw Darryl jump slightly.

'Relax, D. I told you we're just gonna talk. Do you want a drink? I've got better liquor than that shit bar you were in.'

Darryl accepted a glass of vodka and coke and mumbled his thanks.

'How come you were in the club trying to get girls, anyway? I thought you had a girlfriend?'

'We broke up.' Darryl replied, folding his arms.

'How come?' Shorty asked. From what he'd recently learned, Darryl's girlfriend was a beauty. She was a few years younger and had latched onto Darryl, thinking he was a contender on the streets. By the time she realised he was a pretender, it was too late. It seemed she'd found a way out.

'She cheated on me. Banged one of my boys. I caught them doing it.' Darryl looked at the ground as he spoke, missing the corners of Shorty's mouth twitching.

'What did you do?' Shorty asked, taking a moment to compose himself. He wasn't especially interested, but Shorty needed the leverage. It was clear Darryl was uncomfortable talking about the situation, but Shorty didn't care.

'I dashed her, and me and Kyle aren't cool anymore.'

'She banged Kyle?' Shorty couldn't believe his luck. They had spent half their night looking for the man to no avail, only to stumble across one of his crew, who had a legitimate beef with him.

'Yeah. They were out in town with the crew. People were drinking, and it just happened. I was meant to be on a move with Deez, but it flopped, so I went home early. Caught them going at it in my bed.'

'You're lying!' Shorty said, eyebrows raised.

'Course not. I wouldn't lie about something like that. She was crying and trying to get me to forgive her, and Kyle was just saying that he was drunk and that she came onto him. Didn't know who to believe, so I cut them both off.'

'You should have smashed his face in. That would have shown him not to mess with you.'

Darryl shifted awkwardly in his seat. 'Kyle's cool. It could have happened to anyone.'

'It didn't. It happened to you. They took the piss out of you because they knew you wouldn't do anything.' Shorty said, not meeting Darryl's eyes, looking past him, feigning deep consideration.

'How do you know? You didn't even know what happened until I told you,' spat Darryl, forgetting who he was speaking to. Shorty allowed it, taking a moment before meeting Darryl's eyes once more.

'Think about it. They just happened to go back and fuck in your bed on a night when they knew you were handling business? It's common sense. I guarantee her and Kyle have been grinding for a while.' Shorty could see the gears in Darryl's head spinning.

'I didn't think about it like that.'

'Course not. You were in shock, and you're a loyal guy.

AMBUSH

When you're loyal, you assume others are the same.' Darryl nodded, smiling weakly as Shorty continued. 'I know about you, D. You're down with your crew, and you do a good job. I've heard people sing your praises, talking about elevating and moving you up. Maybe even getting a piece of your own.'

Darryl's eyes widened, and Shorty knew that he had him. 'Really?'

'Blood, I roll in the top circles in these streets, and people talk. Your name is ringing out because you're reliable. You're about your business, and the money is gonna come. Speaking of which, here, take that.' Shorty slapped several twenty-pound notes on the table, grinning at the speed with which Darryl picked them up. 'That's for your time. But think about it like this. Help my people set up some meetings with your crew. We can end this whole war, and everyone can return to making money. You get the juice because everyone is gonna see that you were in the middle, making things happen and switching up the conflict. It's gonna raise your profile, and the money will grow.'

'How can I help?' Darryl said, nodding furiously now.

'Do you know where I can find Mori? I can arrange a meeting with him and Marcus, and we can get everything tidied up.'

Shorty watched as Darryl's shoulders slumped.

'Sorry, bro. I can't help you there. I'm not close to Mori.'

'Kyle then?' Shorty pressed. 'You don't owe him anything. If you tell me the best spots we can find him, we will get what we need out of him. I might even smack him around a bit as well. Teach him not to fuck around with the big dog,' Shorty said, balling his hand into a fist and affectionately knocking Darryl on the shoulder with it.

Darryl grinned, Shorty returning the gesture.

'Sure, Shorty. Sounds good, bro.'

Shorty continued to smile as he straightened. 'Thanks, D.

I'll send one of my guys in, and they'll take the details from you.'

As he turned away from Darryl, his smile faded. Shorty stepped towards the door with purpose, opening it and stepping through.

CHAPTER ELEVEN

DARRYL QUICKLY PROVED to be an invaluable resource. He'd given Shorty's people enough information to do serious damage to Mori's organisation. From safe houses to storage facilities, Darryl had come good. It was far more than Shorty had hoped for, and he soon realised that having too much information was as challenging as having none.

Stooping down, he picked up a crumpled piece of paper from the coffee table.

'Do you know which of these spots he's likely to be at?' Shorty said, scowling down at the piece of paper.

'I'm not sure, Shorty. He could be at any of them,' Darryl responded, rising to his feet and moving beside Shorty. 'If I had to guess, I would say this one,' he concluded, motioning to the paper with his forefinger.

Shorty nodded, folding up the paper and placing it in his pocket.

'Maybe we need to think outside the box here,' he said, rounding on Darryl.

'W-what do you mean?' Darryl replied, backing up instinctively.

'You said Kyle was fucking your girl, right?'

'Yeah,' Darryl responded, crossing his arms.

'You also said she wanted you back. That she was trying to get you to forgive her.'

Darryl finally met Shorty's eyes.

'Yeah. So what's your point?' he snapped.

'So, what if you forgave her?' Shorty said slyly. Darryl's eyes narrowed.

'I'm not following.'

'She says she's sorry. That she wants you back. I say you make her prove it.'

Darryl's eyebrows rose as the realisation hit him.

'You don't mean . . .'

'That's exactly what I mean,' Shorty responded. 'We use your girl to set Kyle up.'

Darryl stared at Shorty for a moment, his eyes wide. Rubbing his forehead with the back of his hand, he finally spoke.

'I don't know, Shorty. It seems pretty risky.'

'Of course it is. Why should she have an easy ride? She fucked you over. It's time for her to pay back.'

Darryl nibbled his bottom lip.

'But who's she paying here? How do I benefit from this?'

Shorty's eyes narrowed. He took a step forward, standing close enough for Darryl to feel the man's breath on his face.

'She pays me, and I pay you, you get me? Your pockets are full, bro. You can't say I haven't sorted you out. And as for Kyle, when we're done with him, he'll wish he'd never met your girl.'

Neither man spoke for a moment. Darryl's eyes darted around the room, frantically trying to make sense of the situation. Shorty's eyes remained resolutely fixed on Darryl. A moment later, Darryl fished a shaky hand into his pocket and extracted his phone. Navigating through his contacts, he stopped when he saw *Natasha*, his thumb hovering over the call button. Meeting Shorty's eyes, he pressed it. The phone rang twice before she answered.

———

Natasha needed little convincing. She was clearly sorry for what had happened, and Darryl was obviously relieved to have a reason to abandon his principles and forgive her. Everybody benefited from the arrangement.

After Natasha told Shorty's people which property Kyle was taking her to, the information was relayed to Marcus and K-Bar who hurried to the spot.

Victor parked down the road from the house, the three of them observing the place. It had a dark green door that blinked in and out of sight beneath the flickering streetlight. The brickwork was pale, and there were several plants dotted around the garden. The only light in the house shone from the upstairs bedroom. A sign that things were going to plan.

Opening their doors and closing them quietly, Marcus and K-Bar approached the house. Looking up and down the street, Marcus dipped his hands in his pockets, pulling out a pair of gloves and placing them on his hands. Grabbing the door handle, he pulled down softly, smiling when he heard it click open. Natasha had followed Darryl's instructions expertly, he mused.

They walked in, pausing, scouring the dark surroundings to ensure the coast was clear. Stepping forward softly, Marcus inclined his head, motioning for K-Bar to move ahead.

K-Bar did so, taking his time on the creaky-looking floorboards, Marcus following. They moved smoothly, and Marcus was impressed by K-Bar's overall demeanour. His awareness, his instincts and the murderous look in his eyes. He seemed to understand his role with little instruction, and Marcus understood how rare that was.

Shorty had a good one, he thought.

As they got to the top of the stairs, they heard music playing from one of the bedrooms. Marcus knew it was *Usher*, but didn't recognise the song. He signalled with his hand, and K-Bar nodded, kicking open the door.

The room was dimly lit by several candles dotted around the room, creating mood lighting. Next to the window, a lamp sat, shining out onto the street. There were clothes on the floor and on the large bed, two bodies writhing around, one on top of the other.

Shock engulfed Kyle's face, quickly giving way to confusion. Looking up at Natasha, he saw not a glimmer of surprise or fear. Looking over her shoulder, she brushed her brown her away from her eyes and smiled.

———

Kyle was enjoying the moment, as Natasha kissed down his body. She had set up the room while he'd taken a shower earlier. The candles were a nice touch, and Natasha had dressed to impress. Black lace cascaded down her body, perfectly accentuated by the thick, black lipstick she wore. She left her mark with each kiss, Kyle's eyes rolling as she ran her tongue along his hip.

She was like a drug, and the more he indulged, the more he needed her.

Getting involved with Natasha had been a mistake. Kyle knew she was his friend's girl, but they hadn't planned it. Harmless flirting quickly escalated, and the pair became physical. They'd slept together several times when Darryl caught them.

Even knowing he'd hurt his friend, Kyle couldn't give up on Natasha. The chemistry between them was too potent. It was a spell they simply could not break.

He closed his eyes savouring the moment and vowing that this time would be the last. That this time he would break the habit.

When the door crashed open, his eyes rounded on the wreckage. The door swung loosely on its hinges, the frame shattered into sharp splinters. Finally, his eyes rested on two dark figures that had entered the room. Recognising Marcus immediately, Kyle's face paled.

Looking around, Natasha smiled. Turning back to Kyle, she stooped down and kissed him on the cheek. Standing up slowly, she made her way across the room, crossing her arms, trying and failing to protect her modesty.

'Hello, mate,' Marcus said, his eyes focused on Kyle.

'Fuck you,' Kyle replied, injecting some base into his voice. Ignoring him, Marcus turned his attention to Natasha.

'You did good. Get your clothes on, love.'

Kyle glared at Natasha. 'You set me up, bitch?'

Natasha opened and closed her mouth quickly, struggling to find the words. K-Bar's eyes traced from Natasha to Kyle, growing impatient with the interaction. Grabbing a hooded top from the back of the door, K-Bar threw it to Natasha.

'Get that on and get the fuck out of here,' he said.

Natasha scrambled, pulling the top over her head and scurrying out of the room.

Keeping his eyes on Kyle, Marcus reached down, grabbing the jogging bottoms Kyle had abandoned earlier, tossing them at him.

'Put those on. I'm seeing more of you than I want to. We've got some talking to do, so we're gonna take you someplace. If you struggle, I'm gonna break both of your arms.'

Kyle scowled back at Marcus, but obliged. He was in a terrible predicament, and he knew it. Even if he could somehow get past Marcus, he'd have to deal with K-Bar. With a sigh, he dressed without resisting.

Marcus grabbed him and led him downstairs. They paused, watching K-Bar talking with Natasha near the door.

Reaching into his pocket, K-Bar pulled a stack of notes out, flicking through them and handing some to Natasha.

'You did set me up,' Kyle said incredulously, shaking his head.

Natasha didn't respond, her eyes fixated on the floor.

'We're going to drop you off,' K-Bar continued. 'Give that money to your boy. He's earned it.'

Still looking down, Natasha nodded. Placing his forefinger under her chin, K-Bar slowly lifted her head.

'Listen to me. You're in this now. Don't be losing your nerve and doing something you will regret. Whatever rumours you hear, ignore them. However guilty you feel, swallow it. If you don't, you and Darryl will be in bigger shit than you can possibly imagine.'

'I w-won't say a word. I promise,' stammered Natasha.

'Good, because I've seen your address, so I know where you stay. More than that, I know where each and every one of your family stays, and if you say a word, or if you go near the police, there's gonna be a lot of funerals. Got it?'

Natasha nodded, tears running down her face. Satisfied, K-Bar led her outside, with Marcus and Kyle following.

———

'Did she come good?' asked Shorty, slapping hands with Marcus, K-Bar and Victor as they made their way over to him.

'She did, fam. Absolutely served him up to us on a plate,' K-Bar responded. 'Should have seen the place. Candles all over. Proper romantic shit. He fell for it, hook, line and sinker.'

'Sounds like a keeper. Might have to pay her a visit sometime,' said Shorty. K-Bar's shoulders shook as he chuckled.

'Nah, man. You're not doing that. Stacey will rip your balls off if you go anywhere near her.'

Shorty smirked.

'You're right.'

After a moment, Shorty stepped to the side, rounding his friends and moving toward the centre of the room.

'So, what have we got here then,' he said, looking around K-Bar and Victor. Kyle sat in the middle of the room, tied to a metal chair, wearing nothing but a pair of grey jogging bottoms. A blindfold obscured his eyes, and his head darted left to right, trying to get a sense of his surroundings. His cheek and jaw were already bruised. Dry, crusted blood stretched from his nose to mouth, funnelled perfectly by his philtrum.

'This you?' Shorty asked Marcus, his eyebrows raised.

'Yeah,' Marcus replied simply.

'You couldn't wait 'til we got him here?'

Marcus shrugged.

'He wouldn't do as I say, so I smacked him about a bit.'

Shorty shrugged now, returning his focus to Kyle immediately. Marcus's eyes followed suit as he stepped forward.

'Right, down to business,' he said, the room suddenly standing to attention. 'How are we handling this?'

'We could just take it in turns. Whoever breaks him wins,' said Shorty.

'Wins what?' Marcus's eyebrows rose. Shorty made his way across to the corner of the room. Zipping down his jacket, he fished in the inside pocket, pulling out a small bag full of white powder. Grinning at the others, he placed it on the table, tapping it with his forefinger.

'We're on,' Marcus said, a sinister grin on his face. Moving across to Kyle, he removed his blindfold, crouching down, so he was eye level with him.

Kyle's eyes squinted as they adjusted to the light. He looked around the room, trying to get his bearings. Cobwebs stretched from wall to wall. The exposed brickwork jutted out at curious angles, and the tiled floor was cracked and dusty.

The bright white strip lights contrasted with the dank dark surroundings.

'You gonna talk?' Marcus asked simply. Kyle didn't respond, glaring defiantly back at him. Marcus looked back at the others. Shorty was slouched against the table, smiling.

'Tick-tock,' Shorty said, tapping his finger on his wrist. Marcus turned his attention back to Kyle.

'Where's Mori's people at? I want a list of names, safe houses, home addresses. I want everything.'

'I'm not telling you shit,' spat Kyle through gritted teeth.

Without warning, Marcus straightened up, cocked his fist back and brought it crashing down onto Kyle's nose. The chair tipped over backwards, blood streaming down his face.

As the blood rushed into Kyle's mouth, causing him to cough and splutter, Marcus nonchalantly lifted the chair back up with one hand.

'Let's try again,' he said, 'I want names. You know who I am. You know what I do to people. Make this easy on yourself.'

Kyle's shoulders were rising and falling rapidly, his breath laboured. 'Fuck . . . you.'

Marcus stared into Kyle's eyes for a moment before straightening up once more. Moving across to the table, Marcus removed his t-shirt, folding it and placing it beside the bag of cocaine.

'I've beaten a man to death before. Did you know that?' Marcus said, still facing away from Kyle. 'You know what it's like when you get carried away.' He turned to face Kyle once more, closing the distance between them. 'Or maybe you don't. That's not important. I know what people say about me on the streets. *He's crazy. He's a psycho.* I just call it being good at what I do. Which brings me back to your boss—'

'I told you I'm not saying shit,' Kyle repeated. Marcus turned his head to the side. Opening his palm, he slapped Kyle across the face, his head whipping to the side.

'I'm fucking talking now. Don't interrupt me again.

Like I was saying; people know what I'm about. They know I'm not to be fucked with. I earned this reputation for a reason, so you have to understand I'm not just some little guy trying to gain clout. I can hurt you in ways you've never even thought possible. No one will help you. Nobody's gonna ride out for you. When I finish with you, they'll struggle to identify you.' Marcus walked side to side, prowling like a tiger hunting its prey. Kyle's eyes followed his every move, blood still streaming down his face.

'One of your people gave you up. That's how we found you,' Marcus continued when Kyle didn't respond. 'Your crew is broken. I'm giving you the chance to get out of it in one piece. Your boss and his goons are gonna die for what they tried with me, regardless. You don't have to get caught up in that. The choice is yours, Kyle. What are you gonna do?'

'I told you. I'm not telling you —'

Before Kyle could finish his sentence, Marcus lashed a wicked uppercut under his chin. The chair toppled over once more, Kyle's head lolling to the side. His eyes remained shut as his body impacted the ground.

Marcus turned to the others as Shorty erupted with laughter.

'Fucking hell, he's out for the count.'

'Good, the little prick,' Marcus responded.

'It's my turn when he wakes up,' Shorty said, cracking his knuckles.

Marcus's eyes drifted from his friend to the bag on the table. 'No. I've got him. When he wakes up, you'll see. I saw the look on his face just before I hit him. He's ready to talk.'

'If you say so,' said Shorty, shrugging.

'I'm going to grab a beer. Want one?' Marcus addressed the group.

'Nah, I'm good,' Shorty responded, reaching into his jacket pocket and pulling out a bud of weed. Reaching into his other, he pulled out a grinder, placing the bud in it and twisting side to side.

'I'll have some of that,' K-Bar said, motioning to Shorty.

'Cool,' said Marcus.

Turning on his heel, he made his way past Kyle's limp form and went to grab a drink, placing the beer on the table, as Shorty packed down the spliff. Lighting the end, Shorty took two drags before passing it to Victor.

'How long do you think he'll be out?' Victor said, passing the spliff to K-Bar.

'Not long now,' Marcus replied, eyes fixed on Kyle.

'Did you have to hit him that hard?' said Shorty.

'Yeah. We'd have been here all night, otherwise.'

Slowly but surely, Kyle regained consciousness. Marcus watched as his fingers twitched slowly. His arms pulling hopelessly against his bindings. When he started to cough, Marcus advanced on him, pulling the chair up and fixing him in position.

'Are you ready then?' Marcus asked, slapping him softly on the cheeks.

'If I tell you . . . are you gonna kill me?' Kyle cleared his throat, which did nothing to hide his shaky tone.

Marcus looked past Kyle as he mulled over the question.

'Depends how useful you prove to be. There's no reason to kill more people than necessary. Mori started this. He's the one I want.'

'I can't give you Mori,' Kyle responded, his shoulders slumped.

'Then we have a problem, don't we?' Marcus cocked his fist back once more, watching as Kyle's eyes flashed with fear.

'No, wait! No more, please. I can tell you where Deez is. It's Mori's cousin. He'll lead you to Mori. I don't know where Mori is, I promise. Please don't hit me again.'

Marcus straightened up, eyes still fixed on Kyle. Kyle had validated what Chink had told him. It made him wonder, not for the first time, where he sourced his information from. Shaking it off, he focused. It was clear Mori was wary of giving up his position, even to his own people. Deez was different. Marcus was sure he was the key to unlocking the puzzle.

After a long pause, he nodded.

'Gimme the address and make sure there's no funny stuff. If it's the wrong property, then I promise you you'll be begging me to kill you.'

'It's the right place, trust me. It's just . . .'

'It's just what?' Marcus asked, nose to nose with Kyle.

'Deez is crazy. If you're going at him, go in heavy. Don't take him lightly. He won't give himself up.'

Marcus nodded. 'Thanks for the intel.'

Stepping away from Kyle, Marcus made his way across to the others. Picking up his t-shirt, he pulled it over his head. Reaching for his jacket, he slipped it on and zipped it up.

'Victor, get the addresses from him. Deez is the priority, but we want the addresses for any of Mori's spots he knows. Don't let him go until we're confident they're legit.'

Victor nodded.

Marcus picked up his beer, draining the contents and placing the empty bottle on the table. Picking up the bag of cocaine, Marcus stowed it in his pocket, glancing at Shorty.

'Guess this is mine,' he said.

'Guess it is,' Shorty replied, grinning at his friend.

CHAPTER TWELVE

AN HOUR LATER, the team gathered in the living room of the safe house. Charlie, one of Marcus's workers, had arrived in the meantime. He'd made the rounds and collected some outstanding money for Marcus. When he called to let Marcus know, Marcus told him to come over, figuring they could use him.

'We have the address for Deez then,' said Marcus, leaning against the wall, overseeing the others. He still felt the buzz from the cocaine earlier. The initial haze had subsided slightly, leaving his mind locked in and focused on the job.

'We've got other places too,' said Victor. 'Me, Sharma and K-Bar can go and check those out, see what's what.'

'I'll go and get Deez then,' said Shorty, draining a beer.

'Take Charlie with you,' said Marcus. Shorty rolled his eyes.

'I don't need any help. No offence, Charlie, but I can handle this myself.'

Charlie shrugged, uncaring. He was broad, with thick arms and shoulders, a slightly squashed nose and cauliflower ears from years spent bare-knuckle boxing for little money. Marcus had found him when he was down and out, putting him down with his team and giving him a fresh purpose.

Marcus shook his head.

'Take him. Either that, or me and Charlie will go, and you can stay here with Kyle.'

'Fine.' Shorty scowled. Marcus smirked back at him.

'Just relax, bro. Do what you need to do to get Deez over here. In the meantime, we're gonna be stretched thin trying to keep track of the addresses we were given. Deez is our shot for Mori, so let's make our lives easier. Cool?'

Shorty and Charlie nodded.

'Cool.'

After touching fists with Marcus, they left.

'How do you wanna do it then?'

Shorty didn't reply straight away, adjusting his position and staring out at the location Kyle had given up.

'We go in there, and do what's needed,' he finally said. He checked his phone to see if there had been any messages, then looked at Charlie to see what he thought.

Charlie nodded.

'Both go through the front, or do you want me to take the back?'

'He doesn't know we're coming. I say we just jump right in,' said Shorty. Charlie looked like he wanted to say something, but didn't. Shorty climbed from the car, ensuring his gloves were in place.

The night was chilly, and he kept his head down. Charlie followed suit without needing to be told.

The smell of damp grass and food being cooked in the houses pervaded the air. Shorty's nostrils flared as the smells fought for superiority. It was unpleasant, but Shorty was locked in, already looking forward to the payoff of his evening's work. They'd get the information out of Deez and go about their way, working to eliminate Mori and the rest of his people.

Personally, Shorty had nothing against Mori. The times they'd crossed paths, they'd been respectful to one another. Shorty had seen him at gambling spots and other functions, and they'd shared drinks and talked shit, engaging in a few games of dominoes.

When he went after Marcus, this changed.

Marcus and Shorty's relationship was bonded by blood. For years, they'd worked closely together as partners. Someone going after Marcus was as good as them going after him.

Both Charlie and Shorty were armed, but Shorty didn't think he would need his gun for Deez. He ignored the dire warnings Kyle had given about Deez being a handful. Two people would be enough, and Deez had no idea who was coming for him.

'The guns are for show,' Shorty quietly said to Charlie, who was dressed similarly: Black jacket, trousers and boots. Charlie again nodded.

Deez was staying in a standard red-bricked terraced house with a marred red door and a collection of dirt masquerading as a garden. No care had been put into maintenance, and the few flowers that lived there had long since died. There was a single light on upstairs; a homing device telling the pair exactly where Deez was.

'Watch my back,' Shorty said to Charlie. He spent a few minutes studying the lock. If Deez had an alarm, he would have to improvise. His jaw tensed as he concentrated, getting the lock free and opening the door.

Quietly, the pair searched downstairs, the stench of body odour overwhelming them. Shorty's nose wrinkled as they went to the kitchen, seeing nothing but dirty dishes and cups piled up, along with a protein shaker. Shorty looked in the

AMBUSH

cupboards, seeing some whey protein powder beside a smaller tub of creatine. Closing the cupboard quietly, Shorty returned to the front door.

Grinning with anticipation, he trod up the stairs, Charlie right behind him. The carpeted stairs dipped under his feet, but he kept the sound to a minimum. A television was playing in one of the rooms. *This was too easy*, he thought, already completing the mission in his mind.

Shorty reached the top of the stairs just as a figure charged out. Charlie shouted in alarm, but Deez had already crashed into Shorty, sending him hurtling backwards into Charlie, causing the pair to tumble down the stairs, landing awkwardly at the bottom.

'Fuckers,' growled Deez. 'You think I wasn't ready? My spotter warned me that two dickheads were sitting outside my house. I've been waiting for you to get the balls to come in.' He rushed down the stairs.

Charlie was the first man to his feet, growling and leaping for Deez. There was little room on the cramped staircase, but there was enough for Deez to dodge his sloppily executed jab, slamming his fist into Charlie's stomach, then kneeing the man in the balls. Charlie fell with a groan, and Deez stepped over him, lumbering toward the wincing Shorty, who backed up into the living room. He needed more space to operate, convinced it would help him best his onrushing foe.

He'd got lucky with Charlie, Shorty mused.

'C'mon then, dickhead. I'm glad you know who's come for you,' he taunted.

Deez smiled grimly in return.

'You're gonna regret it.'

The two titans clashed, charging one another. This time, Shorty had his feet planted and saw the move coming, but Deez still knocked him backwards, causing Shorty to hit his lower back on Deez's shabby coffee table, which broke under his weight. He kicked out and sent Deez back, then jumped to his feet, aiming two short hooks at Deez's face.

The first one staggered the bigger man, but Deez shook off the second with surprising ease. He got in close, attacking Shorty with several knees and short sharp hits. The blows were punishing, and for the first time, Shorty wondered if he'd bitten off more than he could chew as he dodged a wild haymaker that may well have decapitated him.

Ducking another hit, he planted his shoulder into Deez's chest and charged, slamming him against the wall. Gasping slightly, Deez gathered himself, driving his elbow into Shorty's back, causing him to fall to his knees. Shorty heard a noise behind him as Charlie entered, looking at his accomplice. His momentary lapse in concentration was all Deez needed.

Deez's hit rocked Shorty's jaw. He sailed backwards, hitting the ground hard, his head ringing as he, again, tried gathering his bearings. He'd never been hit so hard in his life. His jaw ached as he blinked, trying to clear the cobwebs. Charlie was attacking Deez now, who was panting, but still battling on. Charlie got one good hit in, but Deez went to work on his ribs and stomach, the power behind the blows making Charlie's body jerk.

'You two are soft!' Deez roared like some storybook monster. Gripping Charlie's jacket with his left hand, he reared back with his right, his fist detonating against Charlie's jaw. Shorty saw his gun on the floor as Charlie's eyes rolled back in his head. Shaking off the resounding pain, he fired, but his aim was off. The bullet hit Deez in the shoulder, staggering him, but not doing enough to bring him down.

Shorty fired again, but Deez was already on the move, rushing out of the house. Shorty rushed to the door, aiming the gun again, but Deez was already halfway down the road, zig-zagging, making it impossible for Shorty to get an accurate shot off.

AMBUSH

'Fuck,' he hissed, jaw throbbing. He checked his teeth were in place, limping over to Charlie, who was barely moving.

'C'mon, Charlie, we need to get the fuck out of here,' said Shorty. Charlie was practically dead weight, but Shorty got him to his feet. He helped the man to the car, shoving him into the back, shaking his head as Charlie groaned, sprawling out on the back seat.

Shorty jumped into the driver's seat and started the engine, furious. They had failed a simple retrieval, despite having superior numbers. He drove down the street, nostrils flaring.

He wouldn't let this stand. He would settle up with Deez as soon as possible.

CHAPTER THIRTEEN

WHEN MORI HEARD the banging and stumbling outside his spot, he leapt to his feet, fumbling for the gun on the coffee table. When he recognised the loud voice of his cousin, he stilled, remaining standing as Deez barged into the living room.

'What the fuck happened to you?' He asked. Deez had a hand to his right shoulder. Mori's eyes narrowed when he saw the blood. Someone had shot his family.

'Shorty,' said Deez, his eyes gleaming. Mori was nonplussed. His cousin had been shot, yet had a smile on his face. Pushing the fact aside, he told him to remain in place.

'I'm gonna call someone, and we're gonna get them to look at your arm.'

'It'll be fine,' said Deez, gritting his teeth at the same time. He didn't care about the pain. He cared more about what had happened, and the fact he'd not only survived, but taken on two armed men in order to do so.

'Shut up,' said Mori. He headed to the kitchen, grabbing half a bottle of Courvoisier he had stashed there. He handed it to his cousin and told him to drink, Deez doing so willingly.

AMBUSH

Mori made a call, demanding a man with medical experience who owed him a favour to come quickly. Job done, he sat down, watching Deez drinking the brandy like water.

'Slow down on that,' he cautioned.

'I already told you, I'm fine. They tried to kill me, cuz. They came to get me, and I'm still here.'

'Shorty and Marcus?'

'Nah, it was some other goofy dickhead,' said Deez. 'I beat the shit out of him, though. You shoulda been there!'

Mori agreed. This was his battle, yet, Marcus's people had gone for his cousin. Someone had pointed them in Deez's direction, and his first instinct was that it was someone close to them. He would wait for now and gather more proof. Too many hasty moves had been made in his conflict with Marcus Daniels, and he was eager to hold off on making any more.

'Tell me what happened.'

'I was home, and one of the neighbours rang me. Said there was a car outside the house with two guys. They couldn't see properly, but said it looked like they were watching me. So, I waited for them.'

'You waited for them?' Mori couldn't believe what he was hearing.

'Yeah. I wasn't gonna let them send me running from my own spot.'

Mori almost pointed out they'd done exactly that, but didn't.

'Give me the details, stop fucking around. I'm gonna kill Shorty for this,' he vowed. 'I might have given him a pass once I killed his boy, but no more. They're both going down, along with anyone dumb enough to be on their side.'

'Shorty's mine. He's supposed to be tough, but I whacked him up. Waited for him to come up the stairs, then I jumped them. Smacked Shorty around, then his boy, whoever that was. They got a few hits in, but I was amped. I was fucking them up, cuz. We were downstairs scrapping, but Shorty got his gun and managed to shoot me. After that, I got out of there.'

'You did the right thing,' said Mori, still quietly seething. Heads would roll for this. 'Shorty's a prick, but he's good with a weapon. He would have killed you.'

'He's lucky I didn't kill him,' said Deez, scoffing. 'Cuz, I smashed them. Shorty's meant to be a big man who can knock out anyone, but I got him. He's gonna be a laughing stock when I start telling people.'

'Just relax, cuz,' said Mori. 'My contact is gonna stitch you up, and then you're gonna lay low. You can stay here if you like, or I can find you somewhere else. It won't be the best accommodations, but you'll be out of the mix.'

'What do you mean it won't be the best?' Deez scowled, playing with his injured arm.

'I mean what I said. We're at war, bro. I don't have access to as many resources as I'd like.'

'Go see that fucking piggy bank you call a partner. Wisdom has your back. Get some money off him,' said Deez, before shaking his head. 'Doesn't matter, anyway. I need to be out there, letting people know what our enemies are really about.'

A knock at the door disturbed them. Mori grabbed the gun, keeping it by his side. He unlocked the door, looking out at the tall, sandy-haired man in a blue jacket, denim jeans and white canvass trainers.

'Mori,' the man — Brandon — said warily. He had a medical bag in his hand and wore a grim expression. Mori stepped aside. They walked into the living room. Brandon took the measure of the situation in an instant and crouched by Deez, examining his shoulder.

Mori made a cup of coffee in the kitchen, going over things in his head. Having Deez taken out would have been a massive blow. He wouldn't have known immediately either.

Mori wondered what the MO of the opposition was. *Had*

they wanted to interrogate Deez? He wasn't worried if that was the case. Even if they had tortured him, Deez was too loyal to give him up.

Still, he needed to do something.

By the time he finished his coffee and wandered back into the living room, Brandon had stitched up Deez's arm. Other than the wound, he had a few minor cuts and bruises on his face, and looked well for a man who'd fought for his life.

Brandon didn't hang around for long.

'Keep this to yourself. Anyone finds out what you did here, I'll kill you and your family,' Mori said, ushering the man out of the door.

'No one will find out,' said Brandon, wanting to get away quickly. There was a curious look on his face; fear mixed with disgust. Mori closed the door on him. Deez was staring into space. He was shirtless after his examination, his muscled build on show. He had a tattoo of a wolf stretching across his chest. Mori thought it looked ridiculous, but Deez loved it.

'Are you staying here, or do I need to move you somewhere else?' he asked. There was a lot of blood on the sofa. He'd need to do something about that, once he'd made his moves.

'I'm good,' said Deez.

'Okay. I need to make moves. Stay here, and keep your head down. You got lucky, but don't test that. Wait for me to come back, and I'll give you the play.'

'Whatever,' said Deez. 'Just remember, they came for me, and I sorted them out. I'm a soldier, not some pussy who needs to hide.'

Mori could hear his teeth grinding. His cousin's petulant tone irritated him. It was like he deliberately refused to see the big picture.

'I won't be long. I'm not saying you're soft, but you're a target, and you need to chill for a bit.' Touching fists with his cousin, he left.

Deez grinned when Mori left, drinking some more brandy and frowning when he saw it was nearly done. He'd told him what he wanted to hear, but Deez had no intention of sitting around. Reputations were made like this. He'd taken on the great Shorty Turner and not only lived to tell the tale, but he'd won. Something had changed within him. He felt beyond powerful. He'd even taken a bullet. With his newfound notoriety, his rep could even eclipse Mori's, in time.

With that boost would come more money and prestige.

Slowly putting his t-shirt back on, he finished the bottle and grabbed his phone, impatiently tapping his foot until someone answered.

'Yo, where are you? We need to hit town. I've got a story to tell you!'

CHAPTER FOURTEEN

'WHAT THE HELL HAPPENED?'

'Gimme a minute, and I'll tell you,' Shorty said to Marcus, struggling with Charlie, who was still barely conscious and draped all over him. Marcus locked the door, then helped Shorty carry him into the living room.

Lamont was sitting in an armchair. His eyebrows rose when he saw the state of Shorty and Charlie.

'Shouldn't you take him upstairs?'

Shorty shrugged.

'I'll take him later. He's heavy, and I'm knackered.' Hurrying to the kitchen, Shorty rummaged around, grabbing some painkillers and dry-swallowing them. He poured himself a glass of water and downed it. Finding a bottle of whiskey, he took that too.

Marcus and Lamont waited for him in the living room. When he returned, Charlie was stretched out on the sofa, still not moving.

'Do I need to get some help for him?' Marcus asked.

'Yeah, get him some fucking lessons with *Lennox Lewis*. I thought he could fight,' scoffed Shorty, the humiliation from the night still present. He still couldn't believe that Deez had escaped them.

'Charlie's alright. He's proper handy, so I'm wondering how you've both come back looking half-dead,' said Marcus, Lamont hanging back and observing.

'Deez got away,' said Shorty. Marcus shook his head.

'I'm gonna need more than that. Got away how?'

'We watched the spot and broke in. Checked downstairs, and all was well. When we got upstairs, all hell broke loose. He was waiting for us.'

'Do you think Kyle got word to him?'

'He can't have,' Shorty pointed out. 'He's still with our people. It would just make it worse for him. Anyway, Deez said his spotter told him, so they must have seen me and Charlie setting up on him.'

'That's smart,' said Marcus grudgingly, not wanting to give them any credit.

'What happened next?' Lamont interrupted. Shorty shot his friend a glance before continuing.

'We were on the back foot. Bastard pushed us down the stairs, and then we were trying to fight him. He beat the shit out of Charlie and got in some solid digs on me.'

'Looks like he did more than that,' observed Lamont, taking in Shorty's rough state.

'Can I fucking continue?' Shorty snapped.

'Sure,' said Lamont.

'He got some digs in, then went back to destroying that prick on the sofa. I went for my gun to finish him, but he took a shot to the shoulder and kept running. I went after him, but I couldn't get a clear shot. After that, I struggled with Charlie, and we left.'

Marcus mulled over what he'd heard. He was furious that Deez had made a mug of one of his best men. Charlie wasn't soft, which meant that Deez had just been too much for them to handle.

AMBUSH

The door opened, and they all looked up. One of Lamont's workers stood in the doorway, shocked at the state of Shorty.

'I was . . .' he stammered. 'Is that Charlie?'

'What do you want?' Shorty snapped. He didn't have time for this.

'I . . . yo, are you okay?' The man blurted. Marcus smirked, and Lamont rose to his feet, knowing what was coming.

'Shorty—'

'C'mere a sec,' said Shorty to the man. When he was within range, Shorty gripped him, slapping him around the face. The man's legs buckled, and Shorty let him go. 'Get the fuck out here before I tear your head off. Tell anyone, and you're dead.'

'Ted, just go,' said Lamont. 'Take the day off, and I'll come check on you.' He whirled on Shorty. 'I don't care what sort of night you've had. Don't take it out on my workers.'

'He's the one that got in my business.'

'He asked if you were okay. That doesn't give you the right to put your hands on him.' Lamont breathed deeply, shaking his head. 'This is exactly what I didn't want to happen. I wanted to move quietly through Wisdom to avoid this shit show. What the hell have you two been up to? Running around the city, kidnapping people, smacking people around, shooting them. Over what? Mori?'

'What the hell are you getting at?' Marcus asked, annoyed by the lecture. Shorty was bristling with anger and humiliation. If looks could kill, Lamont would be dead.

'I'm saying that this is it. We can't negotiate. That's been made clear. Now, this act means war, all over nothing.'

'It was war as soon as Mori attempted my life, L,' snarled Marcus. 'Sorry that I've inconvenienced your little business deals, but Mori tried to have me killed. He wiped out my team. You need to sort your priorities out.'

'I need to sort my priorities out?' Lamont's voice rose. 'I'm the only one being sensible. I'm not the one charging the streets on a crusade. My role is to ensure everyone makes the most money. You two are my brothers, but that doesn't mean I won't tell you when you're being colossal idiots. You cannot run around like madmen. It's as simple as that.'

'You wanna talk simple?' Marcus glared at Lamont. 'Simple would be me strolling into Wisdom's home, and chopping off his feet, and tearing strips off him until he tells me where his boy is. Why don't I do that, seeing as you can't fucking get anything out of him?'

The friends glared at one another, the tension ratcheting to dangerous levels. Marcus' phone chirping distracted them. Giving Lamont one last look, he answered.

'What?'

'Marcus, it's me,' said Chink.

'Not a good time.'

'I wouldn't be ringing if it wasn't important. You know Deez, right?'

'Yeah,' said Marcus, glancing at Shorty, whose own expression remained thunderous.

'I'm in town, hanging out. I've just seen him in one of the clubs, drinking and throwing money around. He's definitely on one.'

Marcus grinned despite himself.

'Good work. I'm en route now. If he tries to leave, stop him.'

'How the—'

'Text me the club you're at.' Marcus hung up, facing Shorty. 'Look sharp, *Tyson*. Our boy's in town. We're gonna get him.'

'Maybe Shorty should sit this one out,' said Lamont. He was distracted as Charlie stirred on the sofa.

'Fuck that. I'm going. He's not mugging me off and getting away with it,' said Shorty. He hurried upstairs to freshen up, washing and drying his face, then using some cocoa butter he found in a bedroom. Taking off the jacket and undershirt he'd worn, he grabbed a t-shirt and threw it on. Hurrying back downstairs, he signalled Marcus.

'Come. Let's go sort this guy.'

Marcus and Shorty hurried out. Lamont watched them going, still peeved at how things had turned out. He wasn't sure what would have happened if Chink hadn't called, but he refused to hold back with the pair. They weren't thinking about the long-term ramifications of their campaign. All they were thinking about was the release of getting their man.

Lamont was more aware of the powder keg that was Leeds at present. Something was brewing among various factions, and Chapeltown would likely be the battleground for it. He had to keep things smooth, but Shorty and Marcus weren't making it easy.

Closing the door, he went back to Charlie, pulling out his phone. The least he could do was see if Charlie needed more treatment.

CHAPTER FIFTEEN

MARCUS AND SHORTY said little as they headed to the city centre. Marcus drove, Shorty sitting in the back of the car, deep in thought. The humiliation he felt still hadn't ebbed away, the desire for revenge burning within. He was lucky Deez was such a fool. Deez wouldn't get the chance to spread around what happened to too many people.

Not if Shorty had anything to say about it.

'You good?' Marcus eventually asked.

'I should have handled my business.'

'Yeah, you should have. Shit happens, though. Don't let him get by you again.'

'I won't. I've got you backing me instead of Charlie this time.'

'Leave Charlie alone,' said Marcus. 'Deez had the drop on you lot from the get-go. That can't be helped. Charlie has more than handled his business in the past.'

Shorty didn't respond. That was Marcus all over, though. He defended his people as long as they stayed loyal to him. Shorty would let him have it, but he knew that if it had been he and K-Bar, or he and Marcus, the result would have been much different.

AMBUSH

They finally made it into town, immediately besieged by the loud music and flashing lights from the various clubs still open. A few people were on the streets, talking in groups, smoking and drinking, with wary bouncers at various venues keeping their beady eyes on them.

'How do you wanna do this?' Shorty asked, as they got as close to the club as they could.

'I'll go in and look around for him. You stay here and wait for me. I'll drop you a text if they make a move.'

'Nah, fuck that,' Shorty responded. 'I want to be in there. We've got a score to settle.'

Marcus shook his head.

'You know it can't go down like that, Shorty. Deez is a loud mouth. People in there will know what happened – or his version of it at least. If you go in there, somebody is gonna spot you and we'll lose our shot.'

Shorty's face contorted in petulant frustration.

'Well what about you?' he said.

'What about me?'

'You're a big guy. Do you honestly think you can blend in and not be seen?'

'I'll be fine,' Marcus responded. 'I'll lay low and see what's what. If they see me, he'll come outside anyway. Then you can have your fun. Just make sure you don't get seen on any cameras or anything. You know what it's like around here.

Shorty cracked his knuckles now, smiling.

'Cool, bro. Got it. I'll wait out here for the little prick.'

Marcus nodded at Shorty and climbed out of the car. Shorty watched with a moody expression as Marcus strode toward the entrance. The bouncers recognised him and let him straight in, with Marcus slapping hands with them. Shorty recognised the exchange of money and grinned, despite his mood.

Marcus hit the bar and ordered a drink, keeping his eyes peeled for Deez. He was in the moment, nodding his head to the *Heartless Cru* tracks playing, when there was movement next to him. Chink appeared as if out of nowhere. Marcus shook his head at Chink's outfit. He wore a green shirt, brown suspenders with cream trousers, and brown shoes. Somehow, the ensemble seemed to work for him, but there were too many colours for Marcus's liking.

'He's still here,' said Chink. 'He's doing it big in the VIP section. He's been ordering bottles of champagne for him and his lackeys.'

Without making it obvious, Marcus looked to where Chink was directing his attention. Deez was definitely in his element. The big man wore a sling on his bandaged arm, but there was no trace of pain on his face. He was throwing money around, laughing with his friends, a massive grin on his face. This was his moment, and he was making the most of it.

Marcus didn't doubt that the story of what he'd done to Shorty would have been told by now. They'd have to work to ensure it spread no further. When they got Deez, the last thing they needed was Shorty being the prime suspect.

'What a prick,' Marcus muttered, taking a liberal swill of his drink. Positioning himself out of eyeline, Marcus observed the VIP section. Deez had a credit card in hand, furiously tapping it on the table. He lowered his head slowly, jerking it back up at speed. Marcus's eyes widened. Looking down at his drink again, Marcus drained the rest of it. Marcus considered asking Chink if he had a hook up in the club. He felt out of place, and the alcohol wasn't helping to settle his senses.

Before he could ask, Chink nodded at Marcus, mumbled something, and slipped away. Marcus kept his eyes on Deez, but ordered another drink and made small talk with a giggly group of women, who cooed over his muscles.

After what seemed like an age, Deez swigged the remains of a bottle of Cristal, lurched to his feet, belched, and made his way out of the section, followed by two men. The others stayed behind, continuing to drink the bottles they'd left.

Marcus grinned when he saw the men approaching the exit, and fired Shorty a quick text, before keeping his head down and following them.

Shorty grinned when he saw the text from Marcus, and climbed from the car. He watched Deez and two men he didn't recognise stagger from the club. The other men were chuckling as Deez struggled to light a cigarette.

Shorty opened the back door, just as Marcus came out of the entrance, keeping his head down and approaching the group. Without breaking stride, he shoved Deez toward Shorty, catching the man completely off balance.

Shorty saw his chance, a vicious blow landing on Deez's temple, stunning him. Deez recovered quickly, but before he could act further, Shorty's next blow landed right on his injured shoulder, causing him to scream in pain. Shorty pushed and kicked him into the back of the car, continuing to hit Deez when the door was closed, before wrapping a seatbelt around his neck and choking him out.

Outside the car, Marcus had already taken care of Deez's accomplices, with a blow apiece knocking the pair out. Jumping into the car, he drove away just as people converged on the two fallen men.

———

When Deez came to, he found himself tied to a chair in a cellar. He'd been stripped of his clothes, shivering, but his expression as he looked at Shorty and Marcus was intense.

Before he could say anything, Shorty hit him in the face, and Deez felt his nose crunch under the power of the punch. It hurt like hell, but he grunted, willing himself not to show the pain. Shorty hit him again, and again, both times in the face. He pulled back his fist one more time—

'Enough.'

Shorty glared at Marcus.

'Are you serious? This fucker deserves everything he's gonna get.'

'Ask him some questions first. Then smack him around,' suggested Marcus.

'Ask whatever you want. I'm not saying shit,' Deez mumbled. Shorty's eyes flashed, and he moved forward, but Marcus called his name, and again, he stopped.

'Where's your boy at?'

'Which boy?'

'You really wanna take it there?' Shorty warned, an edge to his voice. Deez looked back defiantly. He wasn't scared, despite the imposing figures standing in front of him. Deez was angry with himself. Despite his cousin's warnings, Marcus and Shorty had caught him slipping. He'd foolishly expected Shorty to lay low and lick his wounds after the attack. Gritting his teeth, he stared into Shorty's eyes.

'When I get out of this fucking chair you're de –'

Another sickening blow came crashing down on his cheek, jolting his head to the side. Opening his eyes, he straightened up.

'Just kill me. I'm not gonna tell you anything,' he said, spitting blood on the floor.

Rather than reply, Shorty turned his back on Deez, rummaging around the room. Deez considered using the time to break out of his bindings, but they were tight. He moved his arms slightly, assessing the situation. Between the binds holding him in place and Marcus Daniels looming over him watching his every move, he realised it was hopeless. Deez's eyes moved from Shorty to Marcus, who stood beside him, arms folded, looking down at him casually.

His attention moved again as Shorty clattered around in a drawer, moving his hands around in a frenzy. When he straightened up, Deez saw the screwdriver in his hand, glimmering in the low light.

'Last chance,' he said. Deez glared at him, meeting his eyes.

'Fuck you.'

'Cool.'

Shorty jammed the screwdriver into the side of Deez's left thigh, making him cry out in pain. Shorty twisted the screwdriver, an evil smile on his face, then dragged it out, jamming it into his other leg. Deez let out another cry, jerking in the chair, but unable to gather any momentum.

'You fucker. When I get out of here, I swear you're fucking dead. I'll kill both of you motherfuckers.'

'Where's Mori, and where do his people stay?' Shorty asked.

'You're dead,' Deez repeated, his rough voice racked with pain. 'I've done you once before and I'll do it again.'

Shorty's nostrils flared, his eyes still on Deez. Dropping the screwdriver, he hit Deez several more times in the face. Deez weathered the hits, though he made a noise when Shorty's fist appeared to collapse his cheek.

'Shorty!' Marcus snapped.

Panting, Shorty stopped, picking up his screwdriver and ignoring his friend.

'It's up to you how it goes. I don't give a fuck how much damage gets done,' said Shorty. 'I never had a problem with you before, but you crossed the line when you dared put your hands on me. After that, you thought you could go out and party, like shit was sweet?' Shorty shook his head, twirling the screwdriver between his fingers. 'I bet that champagne tasted good, didn't it? Thinking you'd got one over on me. Thinking I was just gonna sit back and take it!'

The screwdriver went into his uninjured arm this time, right between the bicep. The pain was excruciating, and he cried out, right before Shorty pressed it further in, prying muscle from bone.

This time, Marcus pulled him away.

'Do you want me to take over?'

'I can do this,' snapped Shorty, getting agitated. He focused back on Deez, who was whimpering in pain, his arms and legs leaking blood.

Deez's breathing intensified as he tried to calm down. He didn't want to give them the satisfaction of breaking him, but he'd absorbed a lot of pain, and was struggling to focus. He closed his eyes, his head drooping, but Shorty slapped him awake.

'Oi. We're not done yet.'

The punishment went on. When Shorty had finished poking holes in Deez with the screwdriver, he grabbed a hammer and a set of long, rusted nails. He hammered two into Deez's right foot, and Deez didn't hold back his screams. The screwdriver went into his injured shoulder next. Deez's shrieks faded as his eyes closed and he passed out.

After being doused with water and slapped awake, Deez was forced to look at the pair, when Shorty gripped his chin. He could see the rage and humiliation whirling in Shorty's eyes, but he had no comebacks or insults, just barely keeping himself together.

'Deez, I'm just getting started,' said Shorty. 'Tall-Man over there?' He motioned to Marcus, 'he's getting a bit bored, I can tell. He's not even jumping in to save you anymore. Let me tell you what I'm gonna do next, so you don't have to waste precious energy guessing. I'm gonna stick some nails into your other foot. After that, I'm gonna smash both your kneecaps. Then, I'm thinking I'll jab out one of your eyes,' said Shorty, the screwdriver hovering dangerously close to Deez's face.

'Shorty,' said Marcus.

'I've got this, let me work, bro.'

AMBUSH

He reached for the hammer, and Deez couldn't take it anymore.

'F-Fine,' he said, his throat hoarse. 'I'll tell you.'

Shorty paused, watching him for a second.

'Go.'

Deez spilled. He told them where he'd met Mori, along with two other locations Mori spent time at. He spoke about a few of the men Mori had around him, though he included Kyle in that, not knowing it was he who gave Deez up. When he finished, Shorty looked to Marcus, who had scribbled the information down on a tatty notepad with a pen he'd taken from the bookies.

'How sure are you about these locations?' Shorty demanded.

'One hundred percent,' mumbled Deez.

'I hope so, for your family's sake,' said Shorty. He pulled the nails out of Deez's foot, which again made the man scream in pain. Tossing the nails, then the screwdriver and hammer aside, he began untying Deez.

'Shorty—'

'It's cool, fam,' Shorty said to Marcus, who'd stepped forward when he saw what Shorty was doing. Despite his injuries, a surge of joy flooded Deez's battered body. Shorty was going to let him go, despite everything.

'Stand up,' said Shorty. Slowly, Deez complied, his body groaning with pain, his bruises and wounds numerous. He made it to his feet, but Deez knew he wouldn't stay on them for long. His legs were already trembling as he stood there, but that would pass. The adrenaline would drain away and his wounds would heal. He wasn't embarrassed by the emotions he had shown when he was being tortured, he was simply happy to be free.

'Put your hands up,' Shorty said.

'What?' Deez replied, not thinking he'd heard correctly.

'We've got a fight to finish,' said Shorty. 'You got me

earlier, when you caught me off guard. I got you in town, after I caught you off guard. Now, we're gonna finish it.'

Deez expected Marcus to step in, but he didn't. His muscular arms remained folded, and he seemed content to let it play out.

Deez attempted to raise his destroyed arms, but could barely move them. His legs were already about to give way even before Shorty struck. The blow caught him clean on the chin. Even at full strength, Deez would have been hard-pressed to take it, and in his current position, he had no chance. Falling backwards, his head smacked off the ground.

Shorty mounted him, and the blows rained down, all of Shorty's rage exploding into his punches. Things became fuzzy, and as a solid shot loosened his teeth, the follow-up to the side of the face jerked his head, and he was out.

Shorty didn't care. He didn't care if Deez wasn't moving. He kept on hitting him, throwing flurry after flurry until finally, Marcus pulled him free.

'That's it, Shorty. He's done, man.'

Breathing hard, Shorty rubbed his aching hands, staring at Deez's body.

'Go upstairs and sort yourself out,' said Marcus. 'I'll get the cleanup sorted.'

CHAPTER SIXTEEN

MARCUS AND SHORTY headed back to the spot. Shorty rubbed his knuckles, staring straight ahead, giving Marcus time to analyse the situation. They'd been extremely lucky. If Deez hadn't gone out, they'd have struggled to contain the situation. In the end, they got their man.

He'd been surprised by the ferocity Shorty had shown, and wasn't sure why. Shorty had proved in the past that he would do whatever it took to get the job done, but there was still something distinct and visceral in the way he'd torn Deez apart.

Marcus knew that if he hadn't been with Shorty, the punishment would have been much worse.

Mori would get that message when he learned of Deez's demise.

Lamont waited for them when they arrived at the safe house. He didn't say a word, his eyes flitting between the pair, his expression unreadable.

'It's done,' said Marcus. Lamont nodded, focusing his attention on Shorty, who remained hard-eyed.

'Are you okay?'

Shorty locked eyes with him. 'Why wouldn't I be?' He

looked around the room before speaking again. 'Where's Charlie?'

'He left after I cleaned him up. He's gone home to rest.'

'Rest,' Shorty repeated with a short, high-pitched laugh. 'He needs to work out or something. He was pathetic.'

Marcus shot him another dirty look, but didn't say anything.

'You need to let that go,' said Lamont. 'You sorted it out, so cut Charlie some slack. You could have gone in with anyone, and the same thing would have happened.'

Marcus cleared his throat and raised his hand. Lamont looked confused, but nodded at him.

'I'd have torn Deez's head off. Wouldn't have mattered who I had with me,' he said. Shorty's eyes burned into the side of Marcus's face as Lamont shook his head.

'Let's just stick to the point,' he said. 'Did Deez tell you anything?'

'Yeah,' said Marcus. 'He gave us the location for Mori's main spot. It's in Harehills. He's always there, and so are the people he keeps around him. Deez goes there regularly and gave us the layout. They keep the backdoor locked at all times. There's only one way in.'

'Sounds risky,' Lamont said.

'Yeah, for them. It's dumb boxing yourself in like that. Means they all have to come out the same spot if it gets on top,' said Shorty.

Lamont paused for a second, considering the situation.

'Do I even want to know how you got all of this out of Deez?' he said.

Marcus looked at Shorty, who shrugged, folding his arms.

'I did what I needed to do.'

Lamont's eyebrows rose.

'And what, exactly, does that mean?'

'You know what it means,' said Shorty, puffing out his chest.

AMBUSH

Lamont placed his hand on his forehead and blew out a breath.

'That's not an answer. Just be straight with me.'

'Do you really wanna hear about how I tortured him? Stuck nails into his feet? Beat the shit out of him until he broke?' Shorty snapped.

No one spoke for a moment, Lamont's rosewood eyes boring into Shorty's. Shaking his head again, he finally spoke.

'I guess I don't,' he said. 'Regardless, we need to clean it up. What's the situation with the body?' Lamont rubbed his eyes, blinking rapidly as he opened them again.

'It's sorted. Don't worry,' said Marcus.

'Fine. I'm assuming you have the next steps sorted out for your plan?'

'Someone will watch the spot and let us know when he comes and goes. We'll pick the best spot, go in there and then wipe him out.'

Lamont nodded.

'One thing,' he said.

'Go on,' said Marcus.

'Wisdom is a red line . . . he stays off limits.'

'He's involved,' Marcus growled.

'We're in business together, and we're still making good money with him. Money that makes its way into a lot of pockets. What I'm saying shouldn't be a surprise to you, Marcus. I'm getting sick of having to repeat myself,' Lamont said.

Marcus's rage grew, his eyes bulging.

'So he just gets away with it?' he said, his frustration peaking. It had been a long day, and Marcus didn't need the lecture. He was tired, and the sofa in the safe house was calling to him. As was the bottle of Hennessy he would swill to completion.

As was the bag of white powder he intended to empty.

'You don't even know that he *is* involved, Marcus. You're

just making assumptions and those assumptions are going to get a lot of people into trouble.'

'We can handle Wisdom,' Marcus replied, sneering.

'*We can*,' Lamont said, motioning to the people in the room. 'That doesn't mean everybody can. The second we cut ties with Wisdom, our money goes down. We can ride that out, but it's going to have an impact on our people.'

Marcus took a breath.

'So let's say he is involved. Let's say we prove he was involved all along. What then?'

'If we can prove he's involved, it's different. If he's involved, then you're free to act as you see fit without me getting in the way. People will understand why we needed to take the hit to our bottom line.'

Marcus nodded, seemingly satisfied.

'Did Deez say anything about Wisdom backing Mori?' Lamont continued.

Marcus and Shorty shared a frustrated look.

'No,' Marcus replied.

'No, what? You asked and he said he wasn't involved? Or you asked and he wouldn't answer?'

Marcus and Shorty looked at each other once more. Biting his bottom lip, Marcus responded.

'We didn't ask him.'

Lamont looked from Marcus to Shorty, incredulous.

'*You didn't ask him?*' he repeated. Shorty shifted awkwardly.

'Shit got heavy in there. It's hard to focus when you're in the thick of it. The plan was to get information about Mori, and we did that,' Shorty said.

'You couldn't keep your hands off of him for five minutes longer?' said Lamont. 'So you could validate this wild assumption you're both making?'

Shorty shrugged as the room fell silent.

'He was in a bad way?' Lamont eventually asked. Shorty

nodded. 'If it was as bad as you say, I think he would have offered that information up willingly when you broke him. Him not saying anything could mean Wisdom isn't involved.'

Marcus knew Lamont was right and yet, his words provided little comfort. His instincts told him otherwise. He didn't know to what degree Wisdom was involved, but he would bet a considerable amount on the fact that he was. If he paid Wisdom a visit and went to work on him, he knew he could get the information he needed to prove it.

It wasn't worth the current fallout, though. Lamont was on board with them, and he wasn't stupid enough to throw that support away. As well as being one of his closest friends, a brother in all but blood, Lamont was also fiercely intelligent, and had built an impressive level of resources in his few years in the crime game. It wasn't worth squandering that.

If Wisdom was involved, as he suspected, they would prove it sooner or later.

'So, we get Mori and work him over. If Wisdom was involved, he'll be able to tell us,' Marcus said.

Lamont nodded.

'If you can avoid tearing him apart before he has a chance to speak,' he said, cutting his eyes to Shorty.

'L,' Marcus said, drawing his friends attention. 'If I prove he's involved, you won't be able to save him. It'll be lights out.'

Both men locked eyes, nodding after a few moments. Shorty placed his hand over his mouth, stifling a yawn.

'This is great and everything, but can we get out of here now? I'm tired,' he said, stretching his arms into the air.

Marcus and Shorty left minutes later, Marcus intending to drop off Shorty, dispose of their current car, and then head to one of his safe houses.

When they'd left, Lamont made himself a drink, staring straight ahead and letting out a sigh. Keeping Marcus and

Shorty focused was his hardest job, and there were times he was sure he would fail.

After a moment, he stood and paced the room, analysing everything that had transpired.

There was a lot still up in the air, and he had to keep managing the personalities of the duo.

His ability to do business hinged on that reality.

CHAPTER SEVENTEEN

'YOU WHAT?'

Mori couldn't believe what he was hearing. He stared up at the two men standing in front of him. They looked like they had been through the wars. One rubbed his jaw, where there was livid bruising, growing ever darker. The other had a black eye and still seemed unsteady on his feet. They'd given him the news that Marcus and Shorty had snatched his cousin.

The same cousin he'd told to stay low.

'There was nothing we could do,' one of them protested.

Ignoring him, Mori grabbed his phone. He dialled Deez's number, but there was no answer. Growling, he tried again, growing more panicked. Deep down, he knew that if Deez wasn't answering his phone after what Mori had just been told, he was either dead already or would soon be killed.

'What do you mean there was nothing you could do? You know what he did? Did he tell you about Shorty?'

'He told everyone.'

Mori cursed his cousin's stupidity.

'Why didn't you ring me?'

Both men shared a sheepish look.

'We couldn't get signal.'

'What do you mean you couldn't get signal? You were in the fucking city centre.'

'Well, we nipped back into the club to finish our drinks. I tried to drop you a text, but it didn't send.'

The man with the bruised cheek stepped forward, taking out his phone and showing it to Mori, as if it would help. Mori's eyes flashed with rage.

'Let me get this straight. My cousin was kidnapped, bundled into the back of a car and driven off, and you two went back inside to finish your fucking drinks?'

'We didn't think it was that deep. We knew Deez and Shorty had some shit going on, but Deez is solid. He already fucked Shorty up once.'

'Are you fucking serious?' Mori snarled. 'He got shot. He got the better of Shorty Turner and whatever dickhead Shorty was with. If they're willing to shoot at him, you don't think they're gonna try to finish the job? You don't think it's that deep? Fucking idiots.'

'Sorry, Mori. Really, we are,' the man with the black eye said. His partner made a derisive noise. Mori's eyes shot in his direction.

'You got summat to say?'

Black eye elbowed his friend, but it was too late.

'Yeah, I do. I'm sorry about Deez, but he's a big man, and no one can tell him anything. I mean, didn't you tell him not to go out? That's your family. If he's not listening to you, why's he gonna listen to us?'

It was a good point, but it wasn't one Mori wanted to hear. Standing, he approached the man who'd spoken.

'Maybe you're right,' he said, nodding. Without warning, his fist shot out and caught the man in the same place Marcus had hit him. Bellowing out in pain, he fell to the ground. Mori kicked him several times in the face and stomach, then stomped on his chest, glaring down at him, breathing hard. His partner stood frozen, too scared to get involved.

'Who the fuck do you think you are?' Mori raged. 'I tolerate you lot, but never try to take liberties and tell me what's what. I tell you lot, not the other way around.' He whirled on the man with the black eye, backhanding him and busting his lip. 'And you? Don't just fucking stand there. Get out. Take this dickhead with you and find my cousin. If he's harmed, you two are next.'

Black eye nodded foolishly, helping his partner to his feet, the pair hurrying out.

Mori let out a deep breath, furious. Underneath the rage, his worry grew. Going after Marcus had seemed like such a simple idea. Mori had considered the money he could make from Marcus's rackets and figured he could take over with little fuss.

Not personally going after Marcus was a mistake he still regretted. He would have finished the job and put Marcus down once and for all.

Now, he had anarchy. His men were going missing, or being beaten up in public. Deez was likely dead. There was a chance he'd broken under torture, but Mori doubted it. He knew his cousin. He was strong and loyal. Mori was sure Deez would die before giving him up.

Tapping his foot on the ground, Mori tried to consider his next move. He had people searching all over for him, so his movements were limited. He'd already switched cars, though, so that would buy him some time. Deez hadn't known what he'd switched his car to, which was another positive.

Still, he needed something. He needed to get back on track. With his team slowly being whittled away, he needed the muscle to go at Marcus and his team. Shorty and co were likely involved, so he needed people that could stand with them on an equal level.

Lennox was out. People had already reported he'd been meeting with Marcus, so he was likely compromised.

With a small grin, Mori realised who he'd overlooked. Quickly reaching for his phone, he located a number.

'Ty? It's Mori. Look, I need to see you ASAP. Could be a lot of money in it for you.'

CHAPTER EIGHTEEN

CHINK CLIMBED into Marcus's car. He'd pulled in behind him, the pair parked on Dominion Avenue in Chapel Allerton. Marcus was staring straight ahead when he entered, tapping his fingers.

'Marcus . . . everything cool?' Chink asked. He'd been surprised when Marcus summoned him to a meeting, but had assumed he needed more money.

Not for the first time, he wondered why Marcus didn't just go to Lamont for the money, deciding it simply wasn't worth asking. He dealt with enough politics in his current role without adding the unpacking of Marcus and Lamont's relationship to his workload.

'Yeah. Did you hear what L said about Wisdom? About him being off limits?'

'Yeah, I did.' Chink wondered where Marcus was going with this. He agreed with Lamont for the most part. The team's continued efforts at making money hinged heavily on their ability to do business with outside sources. They traded on reputation, and what they could do for other people, seeking to get the best in return.

Chink didn't doubt they were a more powerful collective

than Wisdom, but Wisdom had allies and relationships of his own, some that intertwined with their own business.

'What do you think?' Marcus asked.

'I think that you're both right. L and Wisdom do business together . . . business that benefits both sides. If you go wading in and kill him, that's going to upset a lot of people. I know you don't fear anyone, but you're still sensible enough not to take on the whole of Leeds when you don't need to.'

'How am I right then?'

'Wisdom needs to be kept in line. If he is colluding with Mori, then all bets are off. Deep down, L probably understands that. If there's proof he's working with Mori, none of his potential allies will stand with him,' said Chink.

'Okay,' said Marcus with a grunt. 'Forget that, anyway. It's not why I asked you here.'

Chink braced himself, wondering how much Marcus would need this time.

'You know my girl, Georgia, right?'

'Yes,' said Chink, flummoxed. 'I've met her before. You introduced us.'

'She's mad at me,' Marcus said, only half-listening to Chink. 'I made her leave the house when all of this popped off with Mori. She's staying with her sister.'

'Were you that worried about Mori going after her? She's a civilian?' Chink pointed out. For the most part, people not connected to the game were left alone when there was a conflict.

Marcus rubbed his chin, finally glancing at Chink for the first time. It struck him just how worn down Marcus looked. He was running on fumes, and Chink could see he was in serious need of a break.

'Those rules don't matter when it comes to some people,' he said.

'Why did you bring her up?' Chink asked, leaving

AMBUSH

Marcus's response alone. Marcus scowled, rubbing his head, exhaling deeply through his nostrils.

'I need you to go and make sure she's okay. Make sure she doesn't need anything.'

Chink said nothing, a bemused expression on his face. He hadn't expected the request from Marcus, and was trying to put the pieces together in his head. Noting his lack of response, Marcus's scowl deepened.

'Spit it out.'

'I'm just thinking . . . you have plenty of people you can send.'

The glance Marcus shot Chink was almost hateful, and Chink fought down the wave of fear that shot through his body at the sight of it.

'Are you saying you don't wanna do it?'

Chink shook his head. 'Course not. I'm happy to help you, Marcus. You know that. I was just curious why you're asking me.'

Marcus's eyes traced from Chink's face down to his feet and then back again.

'You look . . . *different*,' he said.

'What?' Chink asked, unsure if he'd heard Marcus correctly.

'You look different,' Marcus repeated.

'Why? Because I'm white?'

Marcus snorted. 'I know some deadly white boys. No. You look soft. Clean cut, like butter wouldn't melt. Georgia won't be worried about you if I send you to go and see her. So are we good? Are you gonna help?'

Chink fought to hide his annoyance. He knew he was different to the others, but having it blatantly pointed out was offensive and irritating. Holding back his annoyance, he nodded.

'Course I will, bro. I'll go and see her as soon as I can.'

'Take her this.' Marcus reached into his pocket and

handed Chink a bundle of notes. 'She can use it on whatever she wants, and she can contact me or you if she needs more.'

'I'll sort it, Marcus.'

Marcus nodded. Moving too quickly for Chink to react, he grabbed the front of Chink's suede jacket.

'Marcus . . . what the he —'

'Shut it,' said Marcus. 'That's my girl. Don't fuck up, or they'll never find your body. Understand?'

Chink frenziedly nodded, and Marcus let him go, returning to normal as if nothing had happened.

'Cheers, Chink. I appreciate it,' he said, straightening the startled looking man's collar.

―――――

THAT NIGHT, Marcus and Shorty sat in a car, watching the spot Deez had informed them Mori was staying in. They'd had a few youngsters watching earlier, but decided to relieve them of their duties and take over. Though keen and alert, their young eyes lacked experience, and it was experience that would provide the key to unlocking Mori's defences.

Nothing much else was happening, and Lamont had assigned someone to Shorty's duties, allowing him to remain with Marcus until the situation was resolved. So far, they hadn't seen Mori, but had seen several other people who they knew were affiliated with him.

'We should just bust in and take him,' said Shorty, tapping his finger against his leg.

'That approach didn't work well with Deez, did it?' Marcus asked, his eyebrow raised.

'That's on your boy, not me,' Shorty responded, looking out of the window. A smile curled the corners of Marcus's lips.

'Just be patient, bro. There's a lot going on here, and we don't want to fuck up this shot.'

AMBUSH

There were many people coming and going from the spot. The longer they sat there, the more Marcus pondered on Mori's inner circle. Despite their previous efforts to find him, it was shocking that so many people knew where he was, but wouldn't give him up.

Marcus always assumed Mori had a negative reputation. He'd ripped people off in the past and had taken liberties with others. His formidable reputation helped to preserve his life, but he was never truly safe. Over time, as his enemies tried and failed to get to Mori, people became more wary. Outspoken fury turned to disgruntled silence as Mori's status grew.

Marcus wouldn't try and fail like the others before him, he mused. He would get the job done.

Scowling, he thought of Wisdom, and the way he'd acted at the meeting with Lamont. He hoped he was scared now. Marcus had warned him, then had acted as soon as his self-imposed deadline wore off. It was open season on his team.

'What do you think of Sonny Black?' Marcus asked. Shorty stopped tapping, giving the question some thought.

'He's a solid guy. Heard he's good with a knife. There are stories about him cutting people up, but he seems calm. Loyal to Wisdom too.'

'Yeah, that's my thinking,' said Marcus. Shorty glanced at him.

'Are you thinking of taking him out?'

'Might have to,' said Marcus. 'He was at that meeting with Wisdom, and he heard me making threats. He made a few movements like he wanted to get to me.'

Shorty chuckled. 'Sonny's brave, but he's not that brave. He'd need an army to come after you.'

'Wisdom might get him one,' Marcus said. Shorty's eyebrow rose.

'You think it's that deep? You think Wisdom will back him like that?'

'Wisdom's like L. He's about the money. L is backing us in this, right?'

'Kinda,' said Shorty, nodding.

'Why wouldn't Wisdom back Mori then? There's more to this shit than we're seeing, I'm sure of it.'

'You think someone told Mori to come after you?'

'Possibly. I've been in a lot of people's business,' said Marcus. 'My first thought was the yardies. I've done a few things with them, but I went after them hard when they popped shots at you that time.'

'I remember. Never did get the chance to settle up with them for that.' Shorty's eyes darkened. Some months back, he'd been seen around the wrong person. The man was an enemy of the Yardies, which put Shorty on their radar, leading to them shooting up one of his spots. He hadn't been there, but it still angered him. Before he could get involved, Marcus had squashed it.

Marcus was right, though. It was possible that there were still bad feelings from the incident.

'Wouldn't they go after me instead of you?'

Marcus shrugged. 'We don't even know if they're involved. I might speak with Courtney and see if he knows anything. For now, we're on this.' He gestured to the house, where a young man in an oversized hooded top was leaving the spot.

They sat there a while longer. Shorty stifled a yawn, shaking the dregs of the can of energy drink he'd brought along. He checked his phone, reading a text message, then dropped it back on his lap.

'I should have bought more of these drinks,' he said. 'I'm running on fumes.'

'We'll call it a night,' said Marcus. Staying here was pointless. They weren't tailing any of the people coming and going, and to do so would be counterproductive. 'Let's face it: we're not gonna catch him off guard without support, so that means we'll need to hit the spot and hit it hard.' He again looked at Shorty, who was staring past him. 'You listening, blood?'

'Look behind you.'

Marcus turned, seeing two figures who had climbed out of a grey Nissan 4x4. He recognised them immediately.

Tyrone Dunn sauntered toward the house, followed by a man Marcus knew; Rudy Campbell. He watched as the pair knocked. Two men answered.

After a brief conversation, they attempted to pat the pair down, only for Tyrone to slap their hands away. Several seconds later, they were escorted inside. The door closed behind them.

Marcus watched the door a moment longer, then faced Shorty again. The pair shared the same expression. Without a word, Marcus started the engine and pulled away. They had a lot to unpack.

CHAPTER NINETEEN

AS MORI WATCHED Tyrone Dunn being shown into the room, he hoped he wasn't making a mistake. Based on the scowl on Tyrone's face, there was a possibility he was.

This move needed to be made, though. He needed to counter Marcus's crew, and the sad fact was that he couldn't rely on Wisdom. Wisdom was a shrewd businessman, and was good at making money, but he wasn't offering Mori much support in his endeavour. He'd met with Lamont without Mori being around, and he didn't know what else Wisdom was scheming on in the background.

What he did know was, despite offering resources, Wisdom had sent no one his way. Someone like Sonny Black would have been useful in watching out for him. He had lost his cousin and there were reports of others in his organisation going missing too. He needed reliable people, now more than ever.

The Dunns would work nicely if he could sell it.

'Oi, what was your guy on the door thinking?' Tyrone said, his eyes hard. 'Didn't you tell him we're cool?'

'Standard procedure, Ty. You know how it is.' Mori touched fists with Tyrone and Rudy. Drinks were made, and seats taken. Mori considered standing up, but he'd already sat down now, and to get back up would look silly and indecisive.

Mori waited for Tyrone to speak again, wanting him to begin the business first. He and Rudy were happy to sit back, though. Tyrone held his drink, staring Mori down. Rudy sipped his, eyes surveying the room, taking in every detail.

Tyrone and his brother Mitch were established powerhouses in the streets of Leeds. Mitch ran the money, and Tyrone ran the streets. Rudy flitted between both areas from what Mori had heard, doing whatever was necessary. They were hard men, with harder reputations, and he would need to box carefully. He needed firepower, not more enemies.

Tyrone was the broader of the pair, with a heavily muscled build. His facial features were smooth and chiseled. He wore a grey pullover hooded top, jeans and boots.

Rudy was dressed in a black jacket, grey shirt, trousers and shoes. They definitely looked the part, and Mori was impressed, wondering if he should have changed. He rarely felt insecure. He was happy in his own skin and proud of what he had forged for himself. Regardless, Ty and Rudy were symbolic of the life he had settled for under Wisdom. Mori was consigned to perpetual mediocrity; to celebrate minor achievements others in the city wouldn't waste their time with. This was the gift Wisdom had given him. A gift he cherished and resented.

The silence stretched onwards, and realising that the pair wouldn't commit, Mori bit the bullet and went first.

'Thanks for coming. We're all busy people, so I'll skip to the fun shit. Marcus Daniels is a problem. He's attacked my business and has taken out several of my people, for no reason. I want us to work together and take him out.'

Rudy placed his drink on the nearby coffee table, then met Mori's eyes.

'I heard a different story. Heard you tried to set up

Marcus, and that some kids ended up getting killed.' His eyes gleamed.

Mori fought the urge to scowl. He'd hoped they were misinformed about the events, but apparently, someone was keeping them plugged in. He felt the back of his neck heating, struggling to keep his composure. Getting caught out in such a fashion was a major faux pas in street discussions. If he wasn't careful, he would lose their support before he had a chance to gain it. He cleared his throat.

'That was in response to Marcus already making a move. You know what he gets like. He's not all there,' Mori said. 'I think together, our crews can do some damage. He'll never see it coming if we mob up on him.'

'What's in it for me?' Tyrone finally asked. He still hadn't touched his drink. Mori's eyes went from it to him.

'Leeds is a big city. If we get Marcus out of the way, in an efficient fashion, the streets are ours for the taking. We can run wild and make solid money together.'

No reaction. Mori needed to give them more.

'Plus, there's Marcus's little business he's built up. He's got some top-level contacts, and he's making bank through his protection business. It's already set up; I know a few of them well. There might be a couple of stumbling blocks, but nothing we can't handle. Marcus is an idiot, but he's set his business up for success. Anybody could run it. Plug and play.'

Finally, Tyrone sipped his drink, his eyes glinting when he saw Mori take notice.

'Not a bad drink,' he said. 'I'll bring you some better stuff next time. You've said a lot, I'll give you that, but it's all smoke and mirrors. You reached out to us. Do you know what that tells me?'

Mori didn't respond, though he knew the answer.

'It means you need me more than I need you. I mean,

think about it. If I really wanted to knock off Tall-Man, Teflon, Shorty or any of them, what would I need you for?'

'They're not small-timers, that's why,' replied Mori. 'I know what you and your brother are all about, and I'm not trying to pull the wool over your eyes. Together, there are no hiccups. We run them out of the way, and then we take over.'

'What's your boss saying about it?'

'What boss?' Mori frowned.

'He's referring to Wisdom,' said Rudy.

'Course I am. With a name like that, I'd hope he's given you some sensible advice,' Tyrone said, grinning.

Mori seethed. He didn't like the way the conversation was going. He had the distinct impression that Marcus's reputation on the streets was larger than his, and that was tough for his ego to take.

'Wisdom's not my boss. We work together, but I do my own thing,' he said.

'What's he saying about it?'

'He's not saying anything,' said Mori. Somehow, he needed to salvage the conversation. He'd already given more concessions than he'd wanted to. Mori had gone after Marcus for the kudos and, more importantly, to take over his business. He already had to give Wisdom a piece, and didn't want to have to cut the Dunns in too.

'Look,' Mori said, before they could speak, 'the fact of the matter is that we can help each other. I've heard whispers about the moves you want to make, Tyrone. I can help you with that, and you can help me with this.'

Tyrone's eyes narrowed. 'Call me crazy, but that almost seemed like a threat.'

'How?' Mori's brow furrowed.

'I've heard whispers about the moves you want to make . . .' Tyrone repeated. 'You wouldn't be stupid enough to think you can lean on me by outing my plans, would you?'

'Course not. I didn't mean it like that.'

'Good.' Tyrone swept to his feet. 'Keep your nose out of my business. Don't even think of trying me like you did Tall-Man. If you do, I promise I'll be ready for you.' With a final hard look, Tyrone left the room, Rudy following after a curt nod to Mori.

Mori poured himself another drink and downed it. The meeting couldn't have gone any worse. He considered if it would have been smart to have Wisdom present. At the very least, he could have acted as a deterrent to Rudy.

Mori blew out a breath. He would need a better approach. Finding allies that were the calibre of Marcus would be hard, but he couldn't pull back now. He clutched the empty glass in his hand and stared down at the table, hoping it would provide him with the answers he was looking for.

CHAPTER TWENTY

A KNOCK at the front door caused Georgia to jump to her feet, her heart racing. Angie had gone out and left her alone. She wasn't working for the day, and hadn't expected anyone to show up. Her hands trembled at the idea that Marcus's enemies might have found her. She'd been living in worry since he'd exiled her to her sisters, anxious over what it meant, and what Marcus was up to.

Georgia had known what she was getting into when the pair got together. Marcus had an immense presence, and standing beside him made her feel protected. He was rough and crude, but he had a gentle side, and she enjoyed seeing it in him.

The sight of him with blood on his clothes a few weeks back had stayed with her, though. She couldn't shift past it. Marcus had never hidden what he was from Georgia, and she had noted the respect he gained from other people when they were out. Seeing him injured highlighted the less glamorous side of what he did, which frightened her.

Someone like Marcus insisting she had to move out of her house was huge, and Georgia had no idea how bad this would be in the long run.

The person knocked again, the sharp sound causing her to flinch. She took a deep breath, trying to calm down. Finally, she reasoned that anyone that meant to do her harm wouldn't be likely to wait patiently at the door. She hastened to answer, frowning at the man that stood there.

He was average height, with dark hair, sharp features, and eyes that seemed to stare straight through her. He gave her a small smile that put her at ease immediately. Georgia took a moment to take the man in. He wore a pristine light blue shirt, denim jeans, and brown shoes. The thought that this man might be a danger to her suddenly felt quite ridiculous.

'Can I help you?' Georgia asked politely.

'Hey, Georgia,' the man replied. 'My name is Xiyu. I'm a friend of Marcus.'

Georgia's eyes widened, and she gasped audibly.

'Is he okay?' she asked, sure Xiyu had been sent to deliver her crushing news.

'He's fine,' said Xiyu. 'Do you mind if I come in for a few minutes? I promise I won't overstay my welcome.'

Georgia hesitated for a moment, her nervousness returning. She was wary of inviting somebody into the house and knew Marcus would expect her to take necessary precautions. She thought of the names that Marcus had used around her and the people she'd met in the past, namely Shorty, Lamont, and Victor. She had heard other names mentioned, and had an idea of who the man was.

'Do they call you *Chink*?' she blurted out, instantly embarrassed. To his credit, though, Xiyu again smiled.

'They do. Marcus said you were here, and I wanted to check in on you.'

'I appreciate that,' said Georgia, calmer now. 'Come in.'

She led Xiyu into the living room. Her sister had done a good job with the decor since she'd moved in a year ago. The carpet was plush, and Angie was lucky to find the dark brown coffee table. The rest of the furniture ranged toward darker colours and suited the vibe. Like all the others, the room was surgically clean. Georgia had spent most of her spare time either reading, talking with her sister or cleaning to keep her mind off things.

'Would you like a drink?'

'No, thank you,' said Xiyu. 'I won't disturb you for long. How are you doing?'

'With what?' The question confused Georgia, still trying to get used to Xiyu. He was amiable in a way none of Marcus's other friends were. Lamont was likely the closest, but he seemed different. There was something genuinely nice about him, and he seemed incredibly out of place. He looked more like an accountant than a criminal, and it intrigued her.

'Being here. Being away from your home. I know it's not a simple transition, and there's probably a lot of worry and anxiety. Talking helps.'

'I'm terrified, if I'm honest. Marcus just came and said I had to move out, and I don't even know why. When you came to the door, I thought you might be an enemy,' she admitted.

Chink gave her another smile, this one more sympathetic.

'I can understand that. It's difficult to get used to at the best of times. I probably shouldn't tell you this, but there was a dispute, and someone tried to attack Marcus. He's dealing with it, and he wanted you to be protected during this period.'

'Why did someone attack him?' Georgia's stomach lurched. Xiyu steepled his fingers together, still meeting her gaze. She looked away briefly, but her eyes were quickly drawn back to the man. He had kind eyes, and she found them oddly comforting.

'Greed,' he said simply. 'They wanted something Marcus had, and they were willing to kill him to get it. Some people Marcus was close to got hurt, and it caused a massive issue, as you can imagine.'

Georgia's head span as she tried to make sense of what Xiyu had told her.

'Is Marcus in danger?'

Xiyu looked at her for a moment, and Georgia felt her heartbeat quicken slightly. She enjoyed the fact that he had shared information with her, information that he didn't have to, but she braced herself for what he would say next.

'The man he's going after is dangerous, but Marcus will be fine. He has a lot of support, plus it's him . . . the guy is the strongest man I've ever seen, and he knows what he's doing.'

Georgia didn't know what to say, or what she should ask. She wanted it all to be over so she could go back to her normal life, but she'd received no indication of how long that would take.

'Trust me,' Xiyu said, after she said nothing for a few moments, 'Marcus will be fine. I promise. In the meantime, take this.' He handed her some money, the notes neatly stacked, folded and meticulously bound. Georgia looked at the money, then back at Xiyu.

'What's this for?'

'For whatever you need to use it on. Like I said, Marcus wants you to be looked after.'

'When am I going to see him?'

'I'll ask him, and then I'll let you know. It's risky for him to come and see you at the moment. He wouldn't want you in any danger.'

Georgia nodded. There was a lot she needed to protect, but she appreciated Xiyu's words and support. Xiyu again gave her a measured look, before he spoke again.

'I just wondered something . . . while I'm here speaking to you . . .' he started.

'Go on.' Xiyu's words made Georgia feel more nervous now.

'Before you came to stay with Angie, did you notice anything different about Marcus?'

'Different how?' Georgia frowned, surprised by the question.

'Mood swings, low energy, not much of an appetite . . . more secretive?'

'Marcus has always had a temper,' Georgia said, after mulling over his words. 'He eats more than any two people I've ever seen. Haven't noticed anything energy-wise, but there's plenty he keeps to himself. He doesn't like me prying. Why are you asking? What are you trying to tell me?'

'Nothing,' Xiyu assured her. 'We were talking, and I was curious. I appreciate you speaking to me, and make sure you reach out if you need anything.' After giving her his number, Xiyu surprised Georgia by hugging her. Georgia leaned into the hug, taking a deep breath and feeling calmer than she had in a while.

'Thank you, Xiyu. I really mean it.'

Smiling at her, Xiyu gave her a nod and left. Georgia watched him climbing into a blue Jaguar and driving away. She wasn't sure what to make of everything.

On one hand, she now had confirmation that Marcus was involved in a dangerous situation, with his life seemingly at risk. He'd made her go to her sisters to protect her, and it added to the time she'd seen him with blood on his clothes.

On the other, he'd sent the best person to come and comfort her. Xiyu had given her money and information and had reassured her. She'd liked the way he spoke to her, and there was a tenderness in his words and actions that Marcus struggled to muster. When they hugged, he didn't feel stiff like Marcus did. It was nice, and she found herself wanting to hold the moment, just to keep up the reassurance that everything was okay.

Realising she was still standing in the open doorway, Georgia gathered herself and closed the door. Leaving the money on the coffee table, she resolved to give some of it to her sister later, then went to make a cup of tea.

CHAPTER TWENTY-ONE

THE NEXT NIGHT, Marcus and Shorty sat in the safe house, hunched over a table in the kitchen. There were dog-eared pieces of paper, pencils and small blue pens splayed across the weathered table.

Shorty yawned, picking up a discarded can of energy drink and shaking it, making a face.

'Need to tell Blakey to get more drinks,' he mumbled. 'How long have we been up?'

'Too long,' said Marcus, scratching underneath his left eye. Being in the cramped quarters had caused him to shed his hooded top, his muscular build on display in a grey vest.

'I think we've cracked it, anyway,' said Shorty. 'K-Bar did the last shift. He said the usual faces have been there. Ty Dunn hasn't been seen again.'

This was a relief for Marcus. Tyrone Dunn garnered tremendous respect on the streets of Leeds. Whilst Marcus didn't fear him, he wouldn't tangle with him unless necessary. The list of people he treated in this fashion was small: Lennox Thompson, Tyrone Dunn.

Mori, at one time.

'I wonder how that convo went,' said Shorty. 'Think about

it: If he wanted to work with the Dunns, why didn't he move to them earlier? They could have done the hit on you, and if they had the drop like that crew you killed did, it might have been a wrap.'

'It's true,' said Marcus. 'I nearly reached out to Ty myself after speaking to Lennox. I might give him a ring after we sort this. Find out what Mori said to him, and what he promised.'

Shorty nodded. 'Count me in on that. Be interesting to see what Mori tried, and why it didn't work.'

It was Marcus's turn to yawn. Being cooped up in the safehouse was draining. Mori had completely upended his world, and it was yet another thing Marcus needed to settle up with him.

2001 had been a long year, with conflict after conflict. Some Marcus had been directly involved in, others that he oversaw on the peripheries. Rival gangs vying for position and power.

He wanted to go back to normal and recharge.

Rubbing his nose, he debated whether another line would help perk him up. As quickly as that thought popped into his head, he thought about Georgia: What she was doing, whether she was still angry at him for making her go into hiding. He'd become accustomed to taking drugs when he wanted, having been away from her. That would need to change when they were living together again.

'Yo,' he said to Shorty, 'what's Stacey saying to you about all this?'

Shorty frowned. 'What do you mean?'

'You haven't been about. Has she been on your case about it?'

'Nah, think you scared it out of her when you burst in on us, bleeding all over the place.' Shorty laughed.

'It couldn't wait,' said Marcus, irritated.

'I know, bro. Relax. Seriously, Stace knows the score. I

gave her some cash and told her to stay low-key. What about you? Georgia on your case?'

Marcus snorted, leaning back and yawning again.

'Usual shit. That night, she saw me with blood all over me, so she's worried. I sent her to her sisters until shit calms down, so she's not happy with me over that, either.'

'Women, innit.' Shorty shrugged, grinning. 'What even makes them happy? When we're done with this shit, buy her something nice and give her some dick. That'll sort her right out.'

'It better do. If it doesn't, I'm coming after you,' Marcus joked. Both men laughed, feeling at ease despite their cramped surroundings.

'Fuck you. It's nothing to do with me if you can't handle your woman,' said Shorty. 'Back to this, anyway. I think during the day is best, even though it's riskier. Makes it harder to get away, but they're less likely to expect an attack.'

'They've got no reason to think we're coming, anyway. As far as Mori's concerned, his cousin was a standup guy and would never rat him out to us. He probably won't know what's happening until we're on top of him.'

'Maybe not, but we should have a plan, regardless.'

'We will,' said Marcus. 'We'll go in strong. Me, you, K-Bar, Charlie.'

'Are you sure about Charlie?' Shorty pulled a face.

'I know my guys, blood,' Marcus retorted, annoyed. 'Deez got lucky, and we took care of that.'

Shorty nodded. 'Fine.' He scribbled some more notes on a spare bit of paper. 'Mori's the target, obviously. Malston will probably be with him. We took out Deez, and Kyle is still with us. That Darryl guy probably won't be there, but if he is, he goes too.'

'Sounds good.' Marcus smiled again. It would all be over soon. He allowed himself a moment of levity, ready to move past this drama once and for all. Mori and his team would never see them coming. Even if they did, Marcus and his people would have the firepower to wipe them out completely.

'Are we telling L?' Shorty asked.

'We'll tell him after,' said Marcus. 'If we talk to him about it now, he's gonna get all technical and try to shut us down. This is what we specialise in. We get in there and get shit done. Right?'

'Right!' Shorty smirked. 'I'll tell the others to be here tomorrow. What time are we saying? 7 am?'

'Seven is good,' said Marcus. 'Come, we better get our heads down for a bit. Make sure you set an alarm, so we get up.'

Shorty haphazardly tried to organise the papers, but made the pile worse. Shrugging and ignoring it, he walked away, Marcus following. Marcus collapsed onto one sofa, which sank under his considerable bulk. Shorty lay on the second sofa, staring up at the ceiling, already envisioning the carnage that was about to unfold.

Finally, he closed his eyes and fell asleep.

CHAPTER TWENTY-TWO

THAT MORNING, Marcus and Shorty stood in front of the team. Charlie perched on the end of the sofa cushion. K-Bar leaned against the wall, eyes firmly locked onto Marcus and Shorty.

'Right,' Marcus began, 'I hope you all got some rest, because we have no room for mistakes. Mori is a little prick, but he's dangerous, and I don't want anyone taking him lightly. As you know, he's the prime target. If the rest of them move out of the way or drop their guns, I don't care if you leave them alive, but make sure you secure them. Mori is the one that I want. If you can get him without killing him, then cool.' Marcus grinned evilly. 'I wouldn't mind getting to have a chat with him before he gets buried. If you don't, put a bullet in his head, and another one to be sure. Don't hesitate.' Marcus turned to Shorty. 'Anything you wanna add?'

'Yeah. Make sure your guns are locked and loaded, but don't flash them. Don't put your bally on until you're a few streets away, and keep your heads down where you can. It's early, but there will still be people going to work and shit. When we're done, move out, head to one of the drop spots. You know the drill. Clothes, weapons, everything off. Leave the spot, and don't drive the same cars you came in. We'll get rid of them later. Questions?'

Marcus hid his surprise, but Shorty had impressed him. Marcus expected him to make a passionate speech about killing everyone, but he'd ensured that the team stayed on point instead. It boded well for his future career. As young as they were, it was easy to envisage Shorty at the top at some point in the future.

Thinking of that made him remember Lennox Thompson's words about Lamont, and his potential. He knew Lamont could be cold, and at times, he had a certain aura around him that even Marcus found unsettling, but he didn't know if his friend was ruthless, and that was the fundamental difference between Lamont and Shorty.

Marcus shelved it as K-Bar and Charlie shook their heads and stated they had no questions. They were all on the same team, anyway. If Shorty ascended, so would Lamont and everyone else in the room.

'Good. Charlie, you're driving. Wait until we're in position. I'll give the signal when we're good to start clapping. Don't fire a shot until we have a clear sight of Mori. Understand?'

Again, everyone nodded, rolling out and climbing in the ride. They were driving a rusted blue Ford Escort that they'd picked especially for the job. Charlie drove along moderately. Sat in the back, Shorty's eyes locked with Charlie's in the mirror, and he frowned.

'How have you been since that shit with Deez?' He asked.

Charlie's mouth formed a line. His bruising had cleared, but Shorty could see that his pride was still hurt. Next to Shorty, K-Bar stared straight ahead, in the zone.

'Fine,' said Charlie. 'I shouldn't have let him get the drop on me.'

'No, you shouldn't have,' said Shorty, as if he hadn't been beaten badly by Deez too. 'Be on point and ready for that shit.

Don't let it get you down, though. Deez was a tough bastard, but I paid him back for what he did.'

'I heard,' said Charlie, smiling now. 'People were talking about what his body looked like after you lot were done with him. Sent one hell of a message.'

'We're gonna send another one today,' Marcus vowed. He could feel his heart racing, and took a deep breath, relaxing his muscles.

Marcus would need to work hard, and his body and mind were ready. He'd gathered a solid team, and everyone knew their positions. There would be no stopping them. When the streets heard what had gone down, it would elevate everyone to a new level.

Before long, they drove onto the street where Mori conducted his business. Everyone had their guns out, balaclavas firmly in place. They would need to move swiftly and decisively, hopefully avoiding any nosy neighbours who made an appearance.

The street was silent, with nothing but the sounds of traffic in the distance and the rattling of the low winter wind. It was freezing, but nobody present felt the chill.

They had timed it well. Mori and two of his people pulled up at the spot, just as one of their earlier surveillance teams noted they would. Mori would come early, get things set up and, talk business with his team, then move accordingly. He often conducted meetings from the spot, such as the one he'd had with Tyrone Dunn and Rudy Campbell, and sometimes he left the spot to attend others.

As previously noted, people would come and go the whole time, making early morning the best, tightest window to get him.

Marcus's heart smashed against his chest. Mori was there, climbing from the car, not knowing what was about to happen to him. He made his way to the door. All eyes were on Marcus, awaiting the signal. He had his phone in hand, but wouldn't need it.

He was about to signal for the shooting to begin, when a shot rang out.

Marcus's head whirled to Charlie, who was open-mouthed, as if he couldn't believe what he had done.

There was no time to question him.

Mori moved for cover as soon as the shot was fired. His people pulled out pistols, firing back. Charlie was slow to position himself and was hit twice, his body shuddering before he crumpled to the floor.

Shorty was equal to the onslaught, though, proving his mettle by gunning down one of Mori's men. Marcus took out the other just as the door opened, and one of Mori's men wildly fired a submachine gun, causing everyone to take cover.

Marcus tried to get up to aim a shot at him, but the man was firing on all cylinders, and before long, Mori was out of sight. The man with the submachine gun took a bullet to the arm, but was able to get the door closed.

'Fuck!' Marcus glared down at Charlie, who was unmoving on the ground. He couldn't believe how stupid he had been.

'Come,' said Shorty. 'We need to go.'

'Fuck that. We need to go in there and get him.'

'We can't do that,' said Shorty. 'We only have a rough idea of what could be inside, but we know they keep that spot locked down. Getting him outside was the only chance we had. C'mon!'

Marcus didn't like it, but knew Shorty was right. Shorty jumped in the driver's seat and when the others had climbed in, he took off at speed, leaving Charlie's body by the road.

CHAPTER TWENTY-THREE

NO ONE WAS in a good mood as Marcus, Shorty, and K-Bar trudged back to the safe house. They had followed their agreed protocol and changed clothes, leaving everything connected to them at the drop-off point to be destroyed.

Not much had been said. Shorty cursed Charlie out for messing up their plan, but only briefly. The group were frustrated and anxious. They'd missed their best opportunity to take out the enemy, and their job had just grown exponentially more difficult.

Marcus led the way into the safe house. As they piled into the kitchen, they noticed Lamont and Chink already sitting at the table. Both men had cups of coffee.

Chink glanced up when he saw them. His face looked grave as his gaze swept across the group. Lamont's eyes remained fixed on a crumpled piece of paper in his hand. It was one of several pieces dotted around the table that Shorty and Marcus had used to plot their operation. Marcus felt his ears burn as he watched Lamont mentally scrutinising their plan. Taking a deep breath and shaking it off, he stepped forward, eyes moving between Lamont and Chink.

Neither man spoke. Chink's expression was almost pity-

AMBUSH

ing, but it went mostly unnoticed. With the exception of Marcus, all eyes were on Lamont, waiting to hear what he would say. Finally, he put the papers to one side, then finished his cup of coffee. He looked up, eyes flitting between the trio.

'Your plan says *four* people. I only see *three*.'

Marcus's jaw jutted. He didn't like the setup; the idea that he was having to explain to his superior what had gone wrong.

Lamont didn't have the right to judge him. No man did.

After an awkward pause, he spoke.

'Charlie,' he forced the word out. 'He jumped the gun. Didn't follow the plan, and got taken out because of it.'

Lamont's eyes flashed with anger. Again, it took a moment for him to speak.

'You can't be serious. Charlie's good. You said that. You vouched for him in these sorts of situations, so what the hell did he do?'

'We had the drop on Mori. Everything was in place, but he must have got spooked. He fired off a shot, and Mori got away. He had two people with him. And they popped off. Charlie got clipped. We got the others, but Mori got inside, and we couldn't pursue him.'

'I don't believe this,' snapped Lamont. 'I can't believe you got the drop on him, but couldn't deliver. Most of all, I can't believe you guys cooked up this plan and didn't even consult me. Isn't that why I was brought into the fold? I could have helped with the plan. Strategy, planning and execution. It's what I do better than anybody else, and you cut me out.' Lamont threw the stack of papers. Marcus watched as they floated to the floor. His frustration quickly grew to rage. He didn't like the way Lamont was speaking to him, and after a quick glance at Shorty, Marcus noted the same frustration on his face.

'You don't get it. You've got skills, and you're good at

strategy, L, I'll give you that. The streets are our thing, though, and you're too close to Wisdom. That's why we left you out.'

Before Lamont could speak, Chink stooped down and picked up a piece of paper, shaking his head.

'It was a sloppy plan,' he said, further adding to Marcus's annoyance. 'It left you far too exposed, and you left too much to chance. You could have tailed Mori, got more insight into other spots and picked a better time to get him.'

'Mind your fucking business,' spat Shorty. 'This is fuck all to do with you. Kick back and let the adults talk.'

'L's right, and you know it,' said Chink, ignoring Shorty, causing him to bristle with fury. 'You should have brought us both in. If you had, the plan would have been better, which would have yielded better results. I'm also assuming you didn't speak earlier because you were following your own directive and *letting the adults talk*?'

That did it. Shorty moved for Chink, but Lamont jumped from his chair, which clattered to the floor. He got in between Shorty and Chink.

'No, Shorty. You're not touching him. Not for having an opinion.'

Shorty's nostrils flared as he stared at Lamont, then past him. Chink hadn't moved, but he looked unnerved now, realising he had likely gone too far. Shaking his head, Shorty turned on his heel.

'Fuck this shit.'

Storming from the room, he slammed the door behind him. K-Bar went after him, leaving the trio in the room.

Shaking his head at Marcus, Lamont left too, leaving Marcus and Chink alone in the kitchen.

CHAPTER TWENTY-FOUR

'WELL, THAT COULD HAVE GONE BETTER.'

Marcus cut his eyes to Chink. His and Lamont's attitudes still angered him. They had no right to come in after the fact and try to pull apart what they had done.

Marcus's nostrils flared as he thought of Charlie. It was hard to comprehend what had happened to his once dependable soldier in such a short period of time. It was clear that the beating he suffered at the hands of Deez had changed him. It had damaged Charlie physically, but the mental scars the encounter left were what proved to be fatal.

Charlie was experienced and knew what he was doing. They had been in firefights before and had used their guns. More importantly, he knew when to be composed, and when to wait for instruction. In his final moments, this instinct evaded him.

Marcus would need to see about his family, and make sure they got something for their troubles. It wouldn't replace Charlie . . . nothing would, but it was the best he could offer now.

Chink was still looking at him. Judging him. Marcus sat at

the table opposite and, with a sweep of his massive hand, swept all the remaining papers and stationery onto the floor. Chink remained seated, but the look in his eye had changed. He looked startled and alert.

'How many times do I have to tell you to watch your mouth around Shorty? Huh? You think me and L are always gonna be there for you to run your mouth and hide behind?'

'Marcus, I mean . . .' Chink spluttered.

Marcus shook his head. 'Shut the fuck up and listen for a sec, Chink. I know you and L think you have all the answers to everything, but remember this: I'm a killer. K-Bar is a killer. So are Vic and Sharma. Charlie was a killer too. You know who else is a killer? Shorty. He's one of the best around, so if you wanna stay alive long enough to keep wearing your poncey outfits and to keep shagging every slut you meet in town, you better fix up and stop provoking him.'

Marcus's breathing intensified as he continued to stare Chink down, ensuring his friend got the message. Ensuring he truly understood he was playing with fire.

After a few moments, Chink nodded.

'I'm sorry, Marcus. I don't mean to. He's always on my case, and I can't help but retaliate. You're not wrong with anything you're saying, but something else is also true . . .'

'Yeah, what's that?'

'The fact I've never claimed to be a killer. What I am is a facilitator. I make things happen for people. I get them what they want. Most important of all, I make good money for the team. That includes you, and it includes Shorty.'

'Yeah, I know all of that,' said Marcus impatiently. 'Why don't you just say what it is you want to say, and stop fucking around?'

'Respect goes both ways. Tell Shorty to respect me, and I'll treat him in the same fashion.'

'Fine. Whatever.'

AMBUSH

The silence lingered on for almost a minute before Chink slid to his feet and yawned.

'Want a coffee?'

Marcus nodded. Chink went about fixing their drinks, his back to Marcus as he pottered by the kettle.

'I'm sorry about your friend,' Chink said. 'I know you and Charlie were close, and he was always good to me.'

Marcus blew out a breath. 'I dunno what was going through his mind, blood. We were right on top of them. They didn't know we were there. Mori was so close I could have practically reached out and slapped him in his little ratty face. I dunno why Charlie jumped the gun, but he didn't live long enough to regret it.'

'Mori will know what's going down now. He's definitely going to come back. He has to.'

'I know,' said Marcus. He had given little thought to it, but it was academic. Mori had to work in the same streets. If he allowed Marcus to get away with it, it would affect his bottom line. People who traded on their reputations had to make sure they stayed on point. It was the law of the streets; if somebody hit you and you made it through, hit back harder.

Whatever Mori did, he would need to be ready for it.

'I spoke with Georgia the other day,' Chink said, smoothly changing the subject. 'I dropped money off for her.'

'How's she doing?' Marcus asked sharply. He hadn't even texted her to see how she was. He'd had too much on his mind with everything that had transpired with Mori. *She was probably pissed*, he mused.

'She's scared, bro. I spoke with her, put her mind at ease about what was going on, and let her know you'd contact her as soon as you could.' Chink handed Marcus his drink. Marcus mumbled his thanks. 'Are you planning on seeing her?'

'Yeah,' said Marcus. 'I was gonna call her and arrange a meeting.' He saw Chink make a face. 'Why are you looking like that?'

Chink made a show of stirring his drink, then blowing it.

'Look, it's your woman. I'm the last person you need to take advice from,' he said.

'Just talk, man,' snapped Marcus.

'It might be too risky for a meeting right now. What you need is a few days away from everything, just to lie low. Let Mori hunt for a while, then you can react when you have the lay of the land. Everyone in Leeds knows what happened by now, which means people are gonna be looking sideways at you.'

'I'm supposed to hide?' Marcus snarled.

'You're supposed to take yourself out of the mix, temporarily at least.' Chink put his cup on the table, then reached into his nearby jacket pocket. When Marcus saw the bag of cocaine Chink held, he felt his eyes widen further.

'What the fuck are you doing with that?'

'It was going to be a gift for you. To celebrate you taking out Mori,' Chink said, still holding onto the bag.

Marcus's eyes narrowed, though he felt his fingertips and nostrils tingling at the temptation dangling in front of him. Licking his lips, he gathered himself.

'Hang on . . . you were practically calling me a druggy last time, now you're getting me drugs?'

Chink shook his head.

'I was worried about you, as a friend. I asked you about it, and you answered and said you were fine. There's a time and place for everything. This is the time for you to hang back and let your enemy make a mistake.' He held out the bag. After a moment, Marcus took it from him, placing it on the kitchen table next to his coffee. He took a large sip of the hot drink, savouring the feeling.

Maybe Chink was right.

AMBUSH

'I'll chill for a day or two. That's it. After that, I'm right back to it,' he said. Chink nodded.

'After a day or two on that shit, you might not want to get back to it. Just relax and take it easy. The streets will be waiting for you,' he said. 'Just let me know where you're gonna be.'

'I will,' said Marcus. Chink finished his drink and put his cup on the kitchen top. He touched fists with Marcus.

'I'll speak with L when he's calmed down. I'll stress the importance of his support, and we'll get this all cleared up. Sound good?'

'Sounds good,' said Marcus, draining the rest of his drink.

———

Marcus remained at the table, his empty coffee cup sitting beside the sizeable bag of cocaine. Pushing the cup to one side, he placed a giant hand on the bag, moving it towards him. Delicately opening and tipping it, a brilliant white pile formed in front of him.

Rustling around in his pockets, Marcus took out his credit card. Pinching it between finger and thumb, he went to work, chopping down on the drugs until they formed a fluffy white powder. Manipulating the pile with the card, he shaped the cocaine, forming a long line that stretched along the wood grain. Replacing the card in his pocket, he rummaged again, retrieving a battered-looking twenty-pound note. Rolling it carefully, he placed it to his nose, craned his neck and sniffed hard.

Marcus's head jolted back, his eyes wide, note still in hand. With his free hand, he placed his forefinger on the table, dabbing at the remnants and rubbing it on his gums.

As the bitter-sweet taste formed at the back of his throat, Marcus's phone rang. He picked up the phone, analysing the number. It wasn't one he recognised but, after a moment, he answered.

'Who's this?' he said.

'Marcus, it's Sheldon,' the voice on the other end replied.

Marcus closed his eyes and shook his head. A lot had happened since his run-in with the officer, and he knew, without asking, what the man wanted. When Marcus didn't respond, Sheldon continued.

'How are you doing?' he asked.

'Great. Just great,' Marcus responded.

'That's not what I'm hearing, Marcus.' Sheldon blew out a breath. 'What's going on, man?'

'Oh, you know me, Shel. Just going about my business. Keeping my head down. Not much.'

Sheldon sighed again.

'Marcus, what's going on needs to stop. We can't just keep finding bodies and turning a blind eye to them. Things are getting real messy now.'

'I've got no idea what you're talking about, blood,' said Marcus, eyes on the bag in front of him.

'See, I find that hard to believe. You know I'm connected in the streets. I grew up here. People talk. I'm not your enemy, and you know that. I just need to know that this won't go any further.'

'Who are we even talking about here?'

'You know damn well who we're talking about; Mori. It has to stop.'

Marcus picked at his teeth with his finger.

'Mori Welsh? Yeah, he's a bad guy. You should get him off the streets ASAP . . . before someone else does.'

'Don't fuck about with me, Marcus. I'm not an idiot. What's going on?'

'Isn't that your job to find out?' Marcus asked, growing impatient.

'If you're not careful, I just might,' Sheldon responded, before hanging up.

Marcus looked at his phone for a second, placing it on the table a moment later. Picking the bag back up, he emptied out some more, cutting and shaping it. Looking at his phone once more, he shrugged. Lowering his head, the line disappeared a moment later.

CHAPTER TWENTY-FIVE

THE DAY after the failed hit, Chink drove out to Georgia's sister's house, tapping his fingers along to *The Rolling Stones* playing on the radio. As he pulled onto her street, he parked across the road, waiting for the song to end before climbing out of the car.

The weather was mild, and Chink's outfit was a sign of that. He wore a salmon shirt, navy trousers and black shoes. He pulled his shades up and rested them on the top of his head as he made his way across the road.

Knocking on the door, he waited for Georgia to answer, steadying himself and gathering his words.

GEORGIA RECOGNISED the same knock as last time; six rhythmic taps, the second and last spaced slightly apart. Her heart raced for a moment when she heard it, but not for the same reason as before.

Running a hand through her hair, she opened the door to Xiyu, smiling at him. She surveyed his outfit. He looked as dapper now as he had the first time he'd visited. More *Miami*

AMBUSH

Vice than Chapeltown, Leeds. Georgia considered again how strange Xiyu seemed compared with Marcus's other associates. She didn't think she would ever get used to it.

'How are you doing?' Xiyu asked, taking his sunglasses off of his head and placing them in his shirt pocket. Georgia looked into his warm, hazel eyes. Her smile widened. Despite everything happening, she felt good right now.

'I'm better than the last time we spoke,' said Georgia. 'Your words really helped me. I try not to worry about Marcus as much, and that's made things easier.'

'I can imagine,' said Xiyu. 'I actually came here to see if you wanted to go out for a bit. I know a good coffee shop we can go to.'

'Marcus wanted me to stay here, didn't he?' Georgia's eyebrow rose. She trusted Xiyu, but Marcus had tested her in the past, and she hoped this wasn't a twisted game of his.

'Marcus wants you to be safe,' Xiyu corrected her. 'With me, you'll be safe. A coffee and a chat isn't the same as walking around the Hood in our finest jewellery.' He shot her a wink that made her giggle. 'It's up to you. I'll be just as comfortable talking right here.'

'No, I'm being silly. I'm sorry. Let me get myself together, and we can go.'

'You look fine, Georgia. Trust me.' Xiyu looked into her eyes, and a tingling sensation spread through her body.

'I do, but just give me a few minutes. Sit in the living room, and we can go when I'm ready.'

Georgia hurried upstairs to find an outfit. She hadn't brought a vast selection from her house, not knowing how long she'd be staying with Angie. She found a denim skirt and a red short-sleeved shirt that she quickly ironed and put on, grabbing a jacket to complete the ensemble. Thankfully, she had showered earlier, so after doing her hair, applying a small amount of makeup and a little perfume, she was ready.

Heading back downstairs, she stood in the doorway,

facing Xiyu and spreading her arms out. When he saw her, his eyes widened, causing a flutter in her stomach that she hadn't felt for a long time. She loved Marcus, but it was still nice to have a man look at her like that.

'So . . . how do I look?' she asked. Xiyu stood up and smiled widely.

'Magnificent. Let's go.'

———

Xiyu drove them to a cosy little coffee shop in the heart of Pudsey. Despite being familiar with the local area, Georgia had never seen it before, but fell in love with it immediately. Xiyu led them into a corner booth, making small talk with an elderly waitress as they went.

They placed their orders and sat opposite one another. The coffee shop was one floor, and had a dozen booths similar to this one, along with a few stools opposite the main counter. Only two of the booths were occupied. Lounge music played at a low volume, providing a nice ambience, but not interrupting any of the conversation.

Georgia leant back in the beautiful, butterscotch leather seats and closed her eyes. When she opened them, Xiyu was watching her with a small smile on her face.

'What?'

Xiyu shook his head. 'You look cute, that's all.'

Georgia nibbled her lower lip. 'Marcus wouldn't like to hear you saying that . . .'

'No, I suspect he wouldn't,' Xiyu conceded, 'but I didn't mean it like that. It's obvious you're just happy to be outside. It's sweet. How are you doing, though?'

'Like I said, I'm better than I was before, but I still hope this is over soon. I miss my life, Xiyu.'

Their drinks came. Xiyu thanked the barista and added a

sachet of brown sugar to his cup, before stirring it. Georgia added two sachets of sugar to her own.

'I know you do, Georgia. The situation isn't easy, and you've been magnificent in how you've dealt with it. Marcus knows that. I think he knows he'll definitely owe you a few make-up treats when it's all over.'

'If it's ever over.'

'It will be. That I can promise you. Marcus is sorry that he got you involved. It wasn't his intention, and the problem he's dealing with isn't one he caused.'

Georgia felt a warm feeling at Xiyu's words. It was strange to hear an apology on behalf of Marcus, as she couldn't imagine him ever actually giving one himself. Once again, it startled her just how easy it was to talk with Xiyu. She didn't have the mental gymnastics of working out if a topic of conversation was acceptable. It was refreshing.

'How do you deal with it?'

'With what?' Xiyu asked, confused.

'The streets. The drama. What does your girlfriend think about what you're doing?'

'I'm sure if I had one, she'd be upset, but I'd likely still handle things similarly.'

'Similar, but not the same?' Georgia pressed. Xiyu smirked, then sipped his drink.

'I believe in open communication. If I wanted my woman to move somewhere for her safety, I'd at least want to give her some context.'

Georgia sipped her drink now. She was enjoying this time out. Going for a coffee was such a basic situation, but somehow, this felt more charged. Certainly more exciting.

'Can I ask you a question?'

'You just did,' Xiyu replied. Georgia made a face, and he chuckled. 'Sorry. Bad joke. Ask away.'

'How the hell are you in the same business as Marcus? I mean, I've met some others . . . Victor, Sharma, L, that other guy . . . Charlie.' Georgia noted Xiyu pulling a face when she mentioned the last name, but pushed it aside. 'You're so different from the others.'

'Different how?'

'I don't know. More open, I guess. I don't know you all that well, but I'd say you seem to be more in touch with your feelings than the others. L is probably the closest to you, but there's something more distant about him.'

Xiyu took another sip of his drink before answering. Georgia liked that too. She liked that he was considering her words and questions, and not just blurting out answers.

'I'm closer to L than the others. I knew him when we were younger. We met at a library, funnily enough.'

'You're joking.' Georgia grinned, eyebrow raised.

'No, seriously. We both used to get bullied, and the library was a place that the bullies didn't go. We'd read books and go over mathematical equations and stuff together. Chess too. We'd play chess, but L won most of those games.'

'I just can't imagine it,' said Georgia, stunned at what she'd heard. She couldn't imagine anyone bullying Xiyu, and definitely couldn't imagine anyone bullying Lamont. He always seemed like he was in total control, and she'd seen the respect even Marcus showed him.

'It wasn't the best period, but we persevered. Later down the line, I re-connected with L, and we began working together. He had all the others working with him, and I guess I was always the odd one out because I came on board so late.'

'How did you deal with that?'

Xiyu shrugged. 'The only way I know how. I worked twice as hard as everyone else, and slowly started earning everyone's respect.'

Georgia mulled over Xiyu's words, once again pleased he'd shared them with her. They finished their drinks, and

Xiyu went to the toilet. He returned a few minutes later and sat back down.

'Do you want another drink? Anything to eat, maybe?'

Georgia shook her head. 'I'm okay. You can get something else, though. I don't mind.'

Xiyu had another drink, and the conversation changed. They spoke about their families. Xiyu mentioned he was much closer to his mum than his dad, and spoke about his younger sister.

Georgia mentioned her own upbringing, saying Angie was one of the few family members she was still in touch with. The conversation was easy and fast-paced, as if the pair had been talking for years.

By the time Xiyu paid the bill, and they were ready to leave, Georgia felt like she was floating. They were by the door, about to walk outside, when she grabbed Xiyu's hand.

'Thank you.'

'For what?' Xiyu asked.

'For all of this. For taking me out of the house and keeping me company. You didn't have to do any of that, but you did, and I had a fantastic time.'

'I'm glad. We'll have to do it again soon,' said Xiyu. They headed back to the car, and he took Georgia back to Angie's. As they pulled up, she leaned over and kissed him on the cheek, gazing into his eyes for a moment.

'Thanks again, Xiyu. I'll speak to you soon,' she said, climbing out of the car and heading inside.

CHAPTER TWENTY-SIX

'THE FUCKERS.'

Wisdom sat calmly in his chair, watching Mori pace around the room. He'd turned up a short while ago, seething about what had happened. The story of what had transpired in Chapeltown had already done the rounds, and Wisdom was well aware of the details.

Several people had mentioned Marcus's name, and judging by the panicked fury on Mori's face, that was likely accurate.

From Wisdom's perspective, it didn't bode well. Marcus clearly had support, whereas Mori's allies were dropping like flies.

'I can't believe they had the balls to come for me like that,' Mori growled, his pace increasing. Wisdom's eyes traced down to the floor, watching Mori move backwards and forwards, putting unwanted mileage on his new luxury carpet. Refocusing on Mori, he spoke.

'Tell me what happened.'

'What the hell do you think happened?' Mori snapped. 'They came for me. One of them let off too early. If they hadn't, I'd still be on the fucking floor.'

'Why did they do that?'

Mori pointed a trembling finger at Wisdom. 'You're seriously pissing me off. Back up, and stop asking dumb questions.'

'I have to ask questions so I can ascertain the situation,' Wisdom pointed out. 'Regardless, we need to focus on the positives.'

'Which are?'

'You're alive. You got out of there, so no harm done.'

'He dropped my people, Wisdom. Bizzy is gone. Malston isn't even answering my calls anymore. Deez is dead. Fuck knows where Kyle is.'

'I'm guessing that Marcus and the others got your location from them. That means none of your spots are safe,' said Wisdom. He poured himself a shot of whiskey, gazing at the amber liquid, missing the vicious stare Mori sent his way.

'This is fucking Ty's fault,' Mori muttered, finishing his cigarette. Wisdom looked up in time to see ash dropping to the floor. His mouth tightened, before he focused on the business at hand.

'Ty who?'

'Tyrone bloody Dunn. I made him an offer to team up,' Mori explained. Wisdom scowled.

'Why would you do that? No, first of all, what did he say?'

'He turned me down. Didn't want to get involved, even though I offered him a sweet deal.'

Shaking his head, Wisdom sipped his drink. He took his time, not offering a glass to Mori. The last thing he needed was a drunk Mori on top of an angry one.

'That was idiotic. Why would you let him know your plan?'

'I needed allies!' Mori snarled. 'What the fuck are you doing for me? I'm out there in the world, dodging bullets and making shit happen. You're just sat on your arse watching it play out.'

'What are you getting at?'

'You're supposed to be a genius,' Mori snapped. 'You know what I'm getting at. You're supposed to be supporting me, but what have you actually done? You've given me a few weapons and a couple' bodies for bodyguard duty, but where are you?'

Wisdom took another sip. He was playing with fire, but he needed Mori to accept that he wasn't a punching bag. When Mori's bristling on the spot reached concerning levels, he spoke.

'Firstly, you started this. Instead of bringing me in on the plan, you attacked first, and expected me to get involved after the fact. You haven't kept me informed of anything you're doing. What am I supposed to do?'

'Back me!' Mori spat.

'Did you forget about the setup? I'm supposed to make it seem like I'm playing both sides, remember? It's important I seem impartial to L. That gives us an advantage we need,' said Wisdom.

Mori said nothing at first, his scowl deepening. Wisdom began to worry that not having Sonny Black stationed nearby was a mistake he would live to regret.

Finally, Mori shook his head.

'That's not enough anymore The game has changed. Marcus already threatened you. He's taking out my team. You'll likely be next. No more fucking fence-sitting. Either you're with me, or you're against me.'

Wisdom's eyes locked onto Mori's. Placing his glass on the table in front of him, he rose to his feet. He closed the distance on Mori slowly, stepping across the carpet until he was face to face with his partner. Still holding his stare, Wisdom nodded slowly before speaking.

'I'm with you, Mori,' he said. Nodding back, Mori smiled.

CHAPTER TWENTY-SEVEN

LAMONT AND MARCUS met at a coffee shop in Chapel Allerton. Lamont had extended the invite and picked the location. As Marcus lumbered in, Lamont sat serenely in a seat, sipping a cup of coffee. When he saw Marcus, he smiled.

The location was part of a franchise and was spacious, with a nice selection of wooden chairs and tables, along with other, more luxurious leather seating. Lamont had forgone this, settling for the standard wooden chairs.

Marcus took a seat, struggling to get comfortable as a smiling, round-cheeked waitress approached. She had olive skin, and dark hair pulled tightly into a ponytail.

'What can I get you?' She asked. Lamont drained his coffee.

'Same again for me, please,' he said.

'No problem.' The waitress turned to Marcus. 'And you?'

'A coffee.'

'What kind?'

Marcus's brow furrowed. The woman was looking at him like he was a simpleton. Before the moment could grow more awkward, Lamont interjected.

'He'll have a *Grande Americano,* with milk.'

The waitress smiled and headed off. Marcus shook his head.

'What the hell did you bring me here for?' He grumbled. 'I can barely fit in this tiny seat.'

'I like the atmosphere,' said Lamont. 'It's nice in here, and everyone minds their own business.'

'Everyone minds their own business in Chapeltown,' said Marcus.

'We both know that isn't true,' Lamont replied. Before Marcus could respond, the waitress returned with their drinks. Lamont thanked her and asked her to put it on his tab. After seeing if they wanted anything else, she disappeared. Marcus immediately sipped his coffee and made a face. 'What the fuck is this?'

'I believe they use *Ecuadorian* beans,' Lamont pointed out.

Grumbling, Marcus took another sip, reaching for nearby sachets of sugar and using three.

Lamont watched him, amused.

'When you've quite finished giving yourself diabetes, I guess we should get to it.'

'Yeah,' said Marcus. When he'd finished stirring his drink, he spoke. 'I'll go first. Honestly, L . . . I'm not happy with how things have gone. We go way back, and we've always looked out for each another, but I don't like that you weren't all in from the beginning.'

Lamont nodded, accepting this.

'I could have handled things better. That's a fact. At the same time, you need to accept that business always needs to be considered. None of us do the things we do for free, and we always have to think about the wider picture. That's how we've all kept things working so well over the past few years. We're young and rich, Marcus. There's a process behind that.'

'Okay, fair enough,' said Marcus. Inwardly, he didn't fully grasp the point. Business was important, but not at the expense of reputation. Reputation was the true currency of the streets. As a kid, no one had given a shit about Lamont Jones, but they tripped over themselves trying to meet *Teflon*. He'd resolved to approach the meeting with an open mind, though, and wouldn't push it. 'What happens next?'

Lamont sipped his drink, still looking at ease in his surroundings in a way Marcus could never replicate. He wondered just when it was that Lamont had become so comfortable in his own skin. *Was it the power that came from selling drugs?*

'That part is simple,' he said, smiling at Marcus. 'Whatever you need, you can count on me. You have my full support.'

Marcus was elated, but tried hard not to show it. He took a moment, taking a sip of his coffee before turning his attention back to Lamont.

'What's changed then? Why are you suddenly on board?'

'I don't have faith in Wisdom anymore.' Lamont met Marcus's eyes, both men still holding their drinks.

'Why not?' Marcus asked, after a moment passed without Lamont elaborating.

'The initial meeting we had,' said Lamont. 'I studied him. He was being disingenuous.'

'The fuck does that mean?' Marcus scowled. Sometimes, Chink and Lamont were too alike for their own good.

'He wasn't being honest. He could have got Mori to stand down. He puts enough money in Mori's pocket to have sway over him. But he chose not to.'

'I told you he was sneaky,' said Marcus, his annoyance growing. He was struggling to understand why Lamont had been so difficult considering they had shared the same assessment of Wisdom all along.

'I never refuted it. I've told you before, it's vital to keep those sorts of people where you can monitor them.' Lamont held his cup, unaffected by Marcus's demeanour.

'Do you think Wisdom was behind the shooting in Little London?' Marcus asked.

Lamont shook his head.

'No. That doesn't mean he wasn't aware. Wisdom doesn't do anything unless he benefits from it.'

'Why the hell did it take you so long to come to this conclusion?' Marcus demanded. Lamont shrugged, glancing around the coffee shop.

'Do you want another drink?'

'Fuck the drink. Talk to me, L.'

'Marcus, you've known me since we were kids. I like to take my time and think things through.'

Marcus resisted the urge to wrap his hands around Lamont's throat. They were like blood, but he didn't make things easy.

'I'm gonna have to get him. You know that, don't you?'

Again, Lamont shook his head.

'You can't touch him, Marcus. I mean that.'

'When the hell did you think you could start telling me what to do?'

Lamont looked saddened. 'That's not what's going on, and you know it.'

'Explain it to me then.'

'If you get proof Wisdom made a move, then I promise that no one will stand in your way. Hold tight for now, and we'll focus on rooting out Mori.'

Marcus nodded, his grudging agreement. Mori would do. He liked having Lamont on board. It wasn't worth alienating him, but he would definitely be keeping an eye out for Wisdom.

'Come, let's leave this fucking place,' he said. 'I'm hungry. Need some proper food.'

CHAPTER TWENTY-EIGHT

MORI ROLLED THROUGH CHAPELTOWN, taking his time as he drove through the streets. It was evening, but the roads were still busy. He'd only seen one police car during his ride, and the officers were doing a poor job of looking inconspicuous, meaning everyone doing dirt knew where they were, and how to avoid them. Mori was no different.

As he drove down Francis Street, he noticed a group of guys in their mid-twenties. They were talking in loud voices, one of them serving a customer with a dirty-looking face and tattered clothes. Mori slowed down, observing the transaction through his tinted windows. When the dealer finished serving the sale, he kicked the man in the arse, he and his friends laughing as the sale limped away.

The dealer and his friends turned their attention to the car, one of them pointing at it, glares on all four of their faces. The dealer was shaven-headed, with a scar on his face, visible in the glow of a nearby streetlight. He wore a navy blue Nautica tracksuit and a gold chain. Mori didn't recognise him, but he had his gun ready, in case they made a move.

When none of them did, he drove away. Mori's eyes drifted to his rear-view mirror as the group stepped into the middle of the road. Three of the men cupped their hands around their mouths shouting, the other flipping his middle finger. Mori considered slamming on the brakes, turning around and teaching them some manners. In the end, he decided against it. He had places to go and bigger priorities.

The last week had been a long one. Mori had kept out of sight as directed by Wisdom, surfacing only to attend meetings with his partner. He'd been forced to grudgingly admit that Wisdom was far sharper than he had given him credit for. Despite his suspected double dealings and sneakiness, he had a knack for looking at situations from angles Mori would not have considered.

They'd spent the week working to uncover Marcus's plans. He'd made big moves to neutralise a number of Mori's allies, and Wisdom was keen to see if there was a trail to be followed.

They'd started with Westy, but had no luck there. He had evidently seen the writing on the wall, he and his woman fleeing their spot. It frustrated Mori, but he knew it was only a matter of time before Westy resurfaced. Eventually, he would slither back around trying to do business, and Mori planned to take him out when he did.

Malston was still avoiding his calls, but Mori was sure he was still alive and kicking. Why he was dodging Mori was curious, and he intended to get to the bottom of it when he could.

Kyle was another story. It had been a while since Mori had seen him, and Wisdom had suggested looking into what might have happened. He had swept Kyle's house and found nothing. Dust had accumulated on every surface and it became clear quickly that nobody had been there for some time.

After leaving the house, Mori and Wisdom made some calls, asking if anybody had seen him around. Kyle was flashy and lived for the spotlight. If he'd been active, somebody would have seen him, even if he'd gone to ground.

When those lines of enquiry led to nothing, Darryl was the next logical step. He and Kyle were close; if anybody knew anything, it would be him. When Darryl opened the door to Mori, he instantly took a step back. The fear that clouded his face was telling. Mori's eyes narrowed as they focused on Darryl, his eyes darting side-to-side and his face draining of colour.

'Long time no see, Darryl. You cool?'

'Yeah . . . I'm good, bro. How about you? Erm . . . how's . . . ?' Darryl stuttered a reply.

'Let's go inside, and I'll tell you,' said Mori, in as cheery a voice as he could muster. Evidently, he'd done a poor job, because Darryl looked even more frightened. He didn't have the guts to turn Mori down, though.

It had been a while since Mori had visited Darryl's place. He'd started renting it over a year ago and had turned it into a nice little spot. He had a decent television, a PlayStation with lots of games, and an impressive-looking film and CD collection. Everything was neat and well organised, and the magnolia-coloured walls seemed to suit the light grey furniture.

A familiar-looking woman sat on the sofa, watching MTV base. Her hair was wrapped in a bandana, and she wore a red tank top and black shorts. Mori took a moment to check her out before she felt his eyes on her. When she recognised Mori, she froze.

'Hey, Natasha. Long time,' he said.

'H-Hi, Mori. Are you okay?' She asked, eyes wide.

'Yeah,' said Mori, giving her a long look. She turned away, not meeting his eyes. Natasha was loose, and he didn't like her, but he saw the appeal. Mori knew she'd been cheating with Kyle for the longest time and doubted that he was the first man she'd made a play for.

'Sorry about Deez, fam,' said Darryl, after clearing his throat. He stood behind Mori, not knowing what to do. 'Erm, when's the service?'

'We're working on it,' said Mori. His family weren't pleased about Deez's murder, and though few said it outright, they assumed he'd been killed because of Mori.

'Good. Keep me posted, yeah? What's new, though? I heard about some shit going down with some Asians down in the Saville's. Heard they got into it with some Yardies, and now they're running around firing shots off. You know anything about it?'

Mori glanced at Natasha again. She had her eyes firmly fixed on the television, watching the music video intently. Mori could practically taste her unease, and he liked it. She knew he was staring at her, but she was too scared to show her discomfort. He smirked to himself for a moment.

Darryl cleared his throat, then went to sit next to Natasha. His movements were stilted, as if he expected Mori to tell him to get up. When he sat down, Mori spoke.

'Where's Kyle?'

The words were innocuous, but they had the desired effect. Darryl stiffened, and Natasha dropped the remote she'd been holding.

'I don't know,' Darryl said, once he'd composed himself. Mori almost rolled his eyes. Darryl was a fool if he thought such a weak lie would suffice. Even if he'd sounded earnest, Natasha's body language would have given him away.

'You haven't seen him then?'

'Nah, Mori. Haven't seen him in a while.'

Rather than respond, Mori walked into Darryl's kitchen. He took his time rummaging around, smirking again when he heard the panicked whispers from the living room. Finally, he returned, holding a bottle of red wine. Opening it, he took a sip, avoiding making a face. It was a terrible bottle, but it would do for his purpose.

AMBUSH

Darryl and Natasha hadn't moved. They said nothing when they saw Mori with the bottle, but both looked unnerved. Slowly sipping, Mori began walking around the room.

'Tash, what about you?' He asked softly, after a few moments. 'Do you know where Kyle is?'

'N-No. Why would I?' She replied, after glancing at Darryl. Darryl's eyes were wide as he audibly swallowed. Mori smiled menacingly at Natasha.

'Oh, I think you know why,' he said.

'Mate, I'm telling you, we don't kno—'

Darryl never saw Mori coming. With stunning speed, Mori smashed the bottle over his head. He fell to the floor with a moan, hopelessly pressing on the gash that had opened up. Blood poured down his face and over his hands. Mori rounded the sofa and kicked him in the head, then in the ribs.

'Stop it!' Natasha screamed. Mori fixed her with his searing eyes, and she backed up, terrified. There was no pretence now. Mori's patience had run out. He hit Darryl again and again, ignoring his pathetic pleas for mercy.

'Alright!' Natasha shouted. 'Please, stop hitting him. I'll tell you what you want to know.'

Mori stopped, savouring her fear, and Darryl's whimpers of pain.

'Talk.'

'We s-set him up. K-Kyle, I mean,' she said.

'Stop fucking stammering. Tell me everything, you stupid bitch. This is all your fault anyway,' Mori replied coldly.

Natasha told him everything. She explained how she'd set Kyle up, following Darryl's instructions; how men had come and taken him from the house, and that they hadn't heard from him since.

'Which men?' Mori asked Darryl, who was sobbing on the floor, still conscious, but surrounded by blood.

'Marcus. It was Marcus and his guys,' moaned Darryl.

'Good. Don't suppose you know where any of them are?'

'No, please, Mori. We're sorry, but—'

The rest of his words were drowned out. Mori pulled his gun and put a bullet into Natasha's head, the shot ringing out around the room. She slid back in the chair and didn't move, her eyes still open and her mouth agape.

'No! Tash!' Darryl bellowed. Mori kicked him again.

'Show some fucking pride,' he said. 'She fucked your friend. He wasn't the first, and he wouldn't have been the last. Be glad I'm putting you out of your misery, you little snake.' With that, he fired three shots into Darryl's body. He assessed the damage, smiling to himself. He had learned little he didn't already know, but it was a nice message to send to anyone who thought he was finished.

Taking the time to root through Darryl's collection, he took a copy of Mobb Deep's *Hell on Earth* album.

'You don't mind if I borrow this, do you, Darryl?'

When the dead man didn't answer, Mori smiled and left.

Once back in his car, he drove away at speed, removing the gloves he'd worn the entire time he was in the house. He wasn't sure the petrified couple had even noticed. He called Wisdom on his mobile.

'Darryl's gone,' he said.

'Not over the phone,' Wisdom hissed.

'Don't be such a fanny. You're not *Nicky Barnes*, you prick.'

'Whatever. If you're in the Hood, swing by Gathorne Street. There's a house with a red door. Tef does business there.'

Wisdom hung up. Gathorne Street wasn't far, and Mori made it there in no time. The street was deserted, save for two guys smoking outside a house. Mori found the spot that Wisdom was talking about. It had a red door, but there were no lights on inside, and it didn't appear that anyone had been there for a while. Reversing, Mori stopped in front of the two smokers.

'Oi, have you seen anyone staying in that house down there?' He asked, motioning to the property with the red door. The pair just looked at him and went about their business. Mori pulled out his gun and aimed it at them. 'Well?'

Both men instantly raised their hands in the air, terrified. They were likely a few years younger than Mori, but they were old enough to know better.

'Nah, no one has stayed there in a while. It used to be a rock house,' one of them said, his eyes firmly on Mori's pistol.

'Until when?'

'Until about a week ago. Some dudes cleared out of there, and they haven't been back since.'

Mori held the gun on them a moment longer, then put it down and drove away. He was disappointed at not being able to cause more carnage, but ultimately, he'd done some damage and got his name back out there.

It was a start, but he wasn't finished.

CHAPTER TWENTY-NINE

NEWS OF DARRYL'S death did the rounds in the Hood. It had everyone talking, with people questioning the motive behind the murders. Some assumed it was a personal hit, but those closer to Darryl deemed that unlikely.

Despite the fact he was in the life, he was known to be even-tempered and kind. A fundamentally good guy caught up with the wrong people. His closest friends and family held their own suspicions. It was an established fact that Natasha was bad for Darryl. The trouble that had found him in the past could often be traced back to her. She was a drug that poisoned him. The thing that drew him further and further into the life.

'Was there anything Darryl could have given Mori?' Shorty asked. He was looking out of a safe house window, an unlit spliff between his lips.

Marcus sat on the sofa, eyes closed. He didn't care about Darryl or what had happened to him, but he understood the politics. Of all the moves Mori had in front of him, this was likely the most effective.

'Darryl didn't know shit. He could have mentioned Kyle,

but that doesn't matter. Mori can't do anything with that info.'

'What now?' Shorty asked, turning from the window, eyes on Marcus's massive form.

'Mori wanted to send a message. He wants everyone to know that he's badder than bad. He knows we're coming at him, and he's showing off for the streets. Wants them to be shook. To think he can run up in their houses and kill whoever he wants.'

'Overall, he's still down on the scorecard,' Shorty pointed out. 'No one's seen a trace of him lately. Maybe he just fucks off for good, and this shit disappears.'

Marcus sat up, glancing at Shorty.

'That won't happen. He's gonna scurry around in the shadows and try to pick us off. We need to get him, now more than ever. We can't have him out there like a fucking boogieman, causing carnage and disappearing after.'

The brief silence that followed was punctuated by Shorty's ringing phone. He answered.

'Yo? What? Listen, I'm gonna call someone now. Stay where you are.' Shorty hung up. 'Fuck!'

'What's happened?'

'One of our smaller spots got hit. One dude got shot in the leg. Another is dead. He got wigged.'

'Shit,' said Marcus, shaking his head. 'How much did they get?'

'Around twenty-five grands worth of cash and product. Plus, that spot's compromised now. Feds are gonna be all over it.'

Marcus scratched his arm, then stood.

'We need to call a meeting. L and Chink need to be there. We need to get this shit sorted out.'

'Does Chink have to be there?' Shorty asked, a frustrated look on his face.

'He's an annoying little prick, but he's an asset, Shorty. We need both of them.'

Shorty folded his arms petulantly.

'Fine,' he said. 'I'll call someone to go clear out the spot that got hit. If they can get there in time. After that, I'll get onto the others.' Shorty hesitated, phone still in hand. 'You and L alright now? Shit looked intense between you when we were all together that time.'

Marcus nodded. 'We're good, bro. We cleared shit up. He wants to be involved in the planning . . . now he can have his chance.'

———

LATER, the quartet gathered at Marcus's main safe house. K-Bar was overseeing the streets along with other members of Marcus and Shorty's inner circles.

Shorty and Marcus were hunched over the coffee table in the living room. By Marcus's foot was a carrier bag full of Styrofoam containers. A fork had been forced through the middle of one of them when Shorty finished his food.

'What do we know then?' Shorty asked, yawning. He had a pencil in his hand along with a small jotter he'd bought from a local shop. 'Mori hasn't been back to that spot since the shooting. Police have been questioning people about Charlie, but they're not getting anywhere. Has his family said anything?' he asked Marcus.

'They're upset, but they know the rules. Especially his brothers. I've told them we're going to look after them, and they appreciated that.' Shorted nodded. 'There's one more thing . . . Sheldon called me.'

Shorty's eyes widened, and Chink inclined his head toward Marcus.

'Is he on the case?' Shorty asked.

'I'm not sure. He cares about the hood. I think he takes it

personally when shit goes down here. If I was a gambling man, I'd say he's more interested in peace for the people than an arrest for his records.'

'If he wants peace, that's what we'll give him,' Shorty said, grinning. Marcus smiled back at his friend.

'So, we know Mori hasn't been back to the spot we tried him at. Any news of the others?' Marcus asked. Shorty shook his head.

'K-Bar sent some guys to sweep the other spots that Deez and Kyle gave up. They're dead. No one has been near them in the past few days.' He scratched his eyebrow. 'Tell you what, L . . . we should think about taking over those spots or something. Could be a useful resource in the future.'

Lamont nodded, but said nothing, content to let them continue their conversation.

'I doubt we're gonna get lucky with any more of Mori's people,' said Marcus. 'We've got Kyle, but he knows nothing else. In fact, he might have to go, but that's not important at the minute. The fact is, Mori is a ghost right now. For all the people we saw coming in and out of that spot while we were watching it, none of them are about anymore.'

'We can't just sit around here doing nothing. That little prick has to go,' said Shorty. 'He needs to go quick. I'm not looking over my fucking shoulder for the rest of my life.'

Chink sat quietly, surveying the room. His eyes flicked to Lamont every so often, observing him analysing the situation. He wondered when he would speak, and what he would say when he did. Looking around the room, Chink noticed the others looking at Lamont too. It didn't seem to faze him. He sat, staring directly ahead, fingers laced, absorbing all of the detail. His expression was unreadable, which was no surprise.

'L, you wanna chip in here, fam?' Shorty finally asked.

'We need to get creative,' Lamont said after a few moments.

'Creative how?' Marcus asked.

'What do we know about Mori? Not all the stuff you've said just now, but in general. What do we have?' Lamont leaned forward, eyes flitting between the pair.

'We know that he's close with your mate Wisdom. Does a lot of his collections; makes sure that punters pay on time. He had a lot of pieces under him, and we were able to use and neutralise them. In general, he keeps people at a distance and doesn't like unfamiliar faces. We took out most of his inner circle, and the only family he had in the game was Deez . . .' Shorty grinned. 'He's not gonna be popping back up any time soon, I can tell you that.'

'Okay, what about family *not* in the game?' Lamont asked. 'Do you know where his mum lives?'

Marcus and Shorty shared a look, both shaking their heads. To their surprise, Chink spoke.

'His mum is dead. His dad isn't on the scene.'

There was a pause while the group mulled things over. Shorty looked at Chink, his eyes narrowed. Sensing the energy in the room shift, he chose not to say anything. Lamont's questions about family connections seemed to have galvanised them. After banging their heads against the wall, exploring dead ends, they'd finally latched onto something useful. It was a start, and Shorty was keen to see where it led to.

'There is one person who might lure Mori out,' said Chink, delicately.

'Who?' Shorty demanded.

'His baby mother. I've seen her in some of the clubs in town. She doesn't come often, but when she does, she throws money about. Loves Moet. She's also got a big mouth. I've heard her shit-talking Mori before . . . calls him her son's *dickhead dad*.'

'You've known about her this whole time, and you didn't say anything?' Shorty glared at Chink, who shrugged.

AMBUSH

'I didn't know that civilians were part of the discussion. It's not exactly hidden information. I bet if you went out and asked five people in the hood, three would know that he had a kid.' Chink cleared his throat and continued. 'Based on her frequency, I'm guessing that money comes out of Mori's pocket. I can't see him blessing her regularly, so her trips are likely based on what she can get from him. If you can get to her, you can get to Mori.'

Marcus and Lamont stared at Chink, wide-eyed. Chink had a habit of surprising them. He was so easy to overlook, yet he knew so much about so many people, both in and out of the game.

'You still could have said something sooner,' said Shorty folding his arms, unwilling to let Chink off the hook.

'I wasn't included in any of your discussions, was I?' Chink calmly reminded Shorty. 'You didn't want me around. If I had been, and if you'd made it clear what direction you wanted to go in, I would have happily provided information.'

'Do you know where she lives?' Marcus asked Chink, cutting off Shorty's likely angry response.

'No. I can find out, though. For now, you two lie low again. I'll contact you the next time she surfaces at one of the spots.'

CHAPTER THIRTY

ALMOST A WEEK PASSED. Much of the furore on the streets had died down. Police were still making enquiries into the spate of murders, but they were meeting with the usual resistance. The people that knew who were involved were keeping their mouths shut.

With the main suspects out of the mix, additional issues cropped up. An argument between several dealers and a rival Yardie group turned deadly, with a man getting shot in the city centre. This grabbed the attention of the masses, redirecting the focus to new drama.

Marcus spent his time working out during the day and taking drugs and drinking at night. He considered going to see Georgia a few times, but decided it was too risky. He'd sent her a couple of text messages to make sure she was okay, promising to make things up to her as soon as things settled down. She'd replied, but her responses had been short. It was clear she was still angry with him, and he couldn't blame her for that. She'd been forced from her home because of the feud.

Marcus found solace in the fact that she was safe, even if it meant she was temporarily unhappy.

AMBUSH

Mori was still in the wind, and even Wisdom was communicating less with Lamont. It appeared to the group that Wisdom had finally picked his side.

Just as their patience and confidence in Chink had started to dwindle, he came through for them.

Marcus and Shorty were huddled around the kitchen table in the safehouse. With things moving slowly, they'd started to get edgy. When the front door creaked open, their eyes shot to it, relaxing when they saw Lamont. He sauntered in, carrying a white carrier bag full of takeaway food, smiling. The smell drifted through the air, surrounding Marcus and Shorty. Shorty rubbed his hands together, briefly forgetting his frustrations.

'Finally. I'm starving,' he said, rising to his feet and making his way across to Lamont.

'You're always starving, Shorty,' Lamont responded, placing the bag on the table and stepping aside. Shorty approached the bag, ripping the plastic and extracting the boxes. Reading the writing on one of them, he slid it across the table to Marcus. Opening the box, Marcus dug in, stripping chicken from the bone with his teeth.

After a moment, his phone rang. Wiping his hands on his trousers, he picked up the phone and answered.

'What do you have for me, Chink?' he asked, by way of greeting.

'She's here. I just stopped by one of the clubs, and she's in the spot drinking. Something's different, though.'

'Different how?' Marcus didn't fight his grin. They'd been waiting for this moment all week, and finally, the time was here.

'She's not acting the way she normally does. She's been nursing the same drink for about an hour.'

Marcus didn't care about that. He looked to Shorty, then to Lamont, who was standing by the kettle, his finger hovering above the switch.

'Which club are you at? I'm gonna send someone down there asap.'

Chink told him the name of the club. Marcus said he would call him back and then hung up. Shorty was still watching, waiting to hear what had happened. Marcus smiled at him.

'That bitch is in town. Chink just rang me and said he's got eyes on her right now.'

Shorty grinned. 'Right then. How are we gonna do it?'

'That's easy,' said Lamont. 'Someone needs to go to town and speak with her. A proper ladies' man should get the job done.' Grinning, he looked at Shorty.

Shorty's brow furrowed as he looked at Lamont's grinning face, then at Marcus, who was also grinning. He shook his head.

'Nah, I've got a girl. Stacey's cool, but she won't take that shit.'

'You don't have to do anything. Just speak to her and get her talking about Mori, then we set it up from there. Stacey won't even know, and if she does, just explain it to her.'

'Fuck that,' said Shorty. 'What do you think Georgia would say if that was you? Why can't that dickhead we've got in town right now do it? Or even you, L? You've got game.'

'I've got game, but I'm not in the same league as *Badman Shorty*,' said Lamont, still grinning. 'This has got your name written all over it, bro. Tell you what, though: I'll fund your little excursion into town, so at least you don't have to spend your own money. Cool?'

'Cool,' Shorty grumbled, softening. He would have to keep it low-key, and if Stacey found out, he would have to deny everything.

'Excellent. You two get ready then,' said Lamont. 'I'll stay here, so ring me if you need me.'

AMBUSH

Marcus and Shorty got ready, then headed to town just under an hour later. They took a taxi, then headed to the club, recognising the bouncers and walking straight in. The wave of noise overwhelmed them, though it diminished slightly once the pair grew used to it. The UK Garage tracks playing were a huge hit with the audience, and plenty of people were dancing, lost in the moment.

Immediately, they split up, Marcus heading to a far corner of the club that kept the entrance in sight, and Shorty making his way through the sweaty crowds to find Mori's baby mother, Erica.

After a few minutes, he found her by the bar. To his surprise, she was alone. Shorty looked around for Chink, but couldn't see him. Putting it aside, he stepped into her space.

'Can I buy you a drink?' He asked. Erica looked at him, her eyes roving over his body. She felt like she had seen the stocky man before, but wasn't sure where. He was well-built and good-looking, though his eyes were hard. He wore a simple black t-shirt and jeans, but the clothes looked expensive. Erica quickly identified him as a man with money and was instantly receptive.

Since her argument with Mori, he'd all but cut her off, giving her money directly to buy things for Hector, but not enough to afford any treats for herself. As she had to stretch her money and make it last, it meant she couldn't go crazy in the clubs like she normally did. Consequently, most of her club friends had ditched her when she wasn't buying drinks.

Erica had needed to get out of the house, though. Her mum was reluctantly babysitting, so she'd headed out on a budget and talked her way into the club, promising to make time for the bouncer later. She wouldn't, but he didn't need to know that.

'Okay, babe.' She ordered a Disaronno and cranberry

drink, eyes lighting up when she saw the wad of notes the man took out of his pocket. He quickly paid for their drinks, then led her away from the bar and to a group of private tables against the far wall. These were all either taken or reserved, yet when he sat down at a *reserved* table and signalled for her to do the same, no one batted an eyelid.

'What's your name?' he asked.

'Erica. You?'

'People call me Shorty.'

'What's your real name?'

Shorty winked at her. 'You have to earn that.'

Erica giggled. Shorty was smooth and comfortable in his own skin, which she liked. She'd come across a lot of wannabe players during her time in the clubs. Usually, they crumbled when she applied a bit of pressure, but Shorty seemed like he could handle that.

'Are you here by yourself?'

'My boy is around somewhere, but I saw you and told him to make himself scarce.'

'What made you do that?' she asked flirtatiously, liking the gleam in his eyes. They were still hard, but rather than find it off-putting, Erica found it alluring.

'I don't like to share,' said Shorty simply. 'Drink your drink. We've got a long night ahead of us.'

Erica had the time of her life. Shorty was funny, cracking her up with some of his observations and the stories he told. They spoke about their lives, and he didn't even flinch when she told him she had a child.

Shorty kept the alcohol flowing, and Erica drank the majority, taking advantage, as she wasn't paying.

Finally, she was leaning against Shorty, her head on his shoulder, when he spoke.

'Wanna head out? We can go back to your place and chill for a bit,' Shorty suggested.

'Let's go.' Erica didn't need asking twice. They headed out

to find a taxi. Shorty didn't bother looking for Marcus. If his friend was watching the entrance as they'd planned, he wouldn't need to be told. He would know to head back and wait for Shorty to contact him.

They found a black cab, and Erica slurred the address, then draped herself all over Shorty, mumbling in his ear how sexy he was and what she wanted to do to him. Shorty kept the smile on his face. Erica was attractive, but she was abrasive and came on too strong for his liking. Even if he didn't have a girlfriend, he didn't think he'd have gone for her.

They finally arrived at her house on Sholebroke Avenue. Shorty paid the driver, and they headed inside. Once the door closed, Erica started kissing him, and Shorty allowed it, deepening the kiss and pressing her against the hallway wall. After a long moment, he broke the kiss, looking into her eyes.

'Where's the bedroom?'

Giggling, Erica took his hand and led him to her room. As they went upstairs, he looked for any sign of Mori, but found none. In the bedroom, Erica fell onto the bed, opening and closing her legs, shooting him a sultry grin.

'What now?' She asked softly. Shorty grinned at her.

'Gimme a minute. I'm gonna use the bathroom, then we can get to it.'

Shorty stepped into the bathroom, using the toilet and washing his hands. He looked around the bathroom, again seeing no traces of Mori. Either he wasn't intimately involved with his baby mother anymore, or Erica was exceptional at hiding him. His eyes landed on a bottle of children's bubble bath for a second, then he shook his head.

Shorty stared into the mirror, seeing his disappointment reflected back at him. He'd known when he left for town where the night might lead, but that didn't make it any easier for him now he was here. He liked Stacey a lot, and the thought of betraying her trust hurt him more than he'd expected. But this wasn't about Stacey or Shorty. It was about the crew, and getting the job done.

Shorty took a deep breath, turning the tap on and splashing his face. Avoiding it wouldn't help. Soon, it would all be over, and their plan would be in motion.

He headed back into the bedroom, immediately greeted by the sound of soft snoring. Erica had fallen asleep on top of the bed.

Shorty smiled, slowly rolling her onto her side in case she threw up. Erica murmured, but didn't wake up. Leaving the room, Shorty sent Marcus a text message, giving him the address, and telling him he would let him know when to come. When that was done, he went downstairs and switched on her television, pleased to see she had a chipped cable box.

CHAPTER THIRTY-ONE

ERICA WOKE up with a dry mouth and throbbing head the next morning. Shuffling to her feet, she swayed slightly, taking a moment to steady herself. Lifting her fingers to her temples, she rubbed slowly, desperately trying to rid herself of the intense headache. Once again, she had drank too much, and made a fool of herself.

Coughing to clear her throat, Erica made her way out of the bedroom and headed for the stairs. As she went, she recalled flashes of the night before; the dancing, the drinking and, finally, the man she had met. She wondered where he'd got to. The night was a blur, but she was sure he got into the taxi that took them to her house.

As Erica arrived at the bottom of the stairs, she stopped outside the living room door. Her hand was suspended in front of it, ready to push it open, but unable to act. Erica could hear the television playing on the other side.

After taking a moment to compose herself, she took a deep breath and entered the room. Her eyes flicked from the television to the man she'd met the night before. He was sat on the sofa, coffee in hand and smiling. A moment of panic overcame Erica when she realised she couldn't remember his name. Swallowing down her anxiety, she smiled back.

'Hey . . .' she said.

'Hey, Erica. Thirsty? I can make you some coffee if you want.'

'That sounds nice,' she replied, still staring at him. He slid to his feet and, as she took in his short and stocky frame, she finally remembered his name. *Shorty.*

'How do you want it?'

'Huh?' she asked, nonplussed.

'Your coffee,' said Shorty. 'How do you want it?'

'Ohh. Milk and two sugars, please.'

Shorty nodded and went to the kitchen. Erica sat down, again rubbing her forehead, pleased she didn't feel nauseous. After a minute, Shorty placed a steaming mug in front of her.

'There you go.'

'Thank you. What time is it?' Erica asked. Her mum wouldn't hurry her to pick up Hector, which was a relief, as she needed a few hours to get herself together.

'Just after nine,' said Shorty.

'How come you're up so early?'

Shorty shrugged. 'I never sleep for long. The liquor is probably still in my system.'

'Sorry about last night,' Erica said, embarrassed. 'I must have been in such a state. Don't even remember most of it.'

'Don't worry about it. We had a good time. I wanted to make sure you were okay, though. Didn't want you going home without checking you were safe,' said Shorty.

'Thank you. That's sweet.' Erica meant it. It wasn't her first foray into the club scene, and it wasn't the first time she had taken a guy home with her. In situations like this, people would usually take advantage of her and leave. Shorty seemed different. He had stayed, ensured she was okay, and left her to rest up.

Erica needed the release that the night out afforded her.

Mori had refused to give her any money when she'd pressed him, and had threatened to kill her if she bothered him again without a good reason.

She'd gone out with the money she had, taken her time with her drinks, hoping to run into the right guy. It seemed she'd struck the jackpot with Shorty.

'It's cool. What are you saying, though? How come you were out by yourself?' Shorty asked.

'I just needed a distraction, I guess.'

'Must be man trouble,' said Shorty. Erica went to defend herself, but he shook his head.

'It's cool. Seriously. I get it.'

'What happened last night? I remember meeting you, and I remember all the drinks, but what happened next?'

'We came back here and went upstairs, and then you fell asleep,' said Shorty. 'I put you on your side, so you didn't throw up, and then came down here to chill.'

'Why? Didn't you want to sleep with me?' she quietly asked, her chest tightening.

Shorty chuckled. 'I wanted you awake when it happened. I'm not gonna go after you while your head rocks about the pillow. The second you fell asleep, I knew it just wasn't meant to be. Not last night, at least,' he said, smiling warmly.

Despite her rough condition, a searing heat spread through her body, both at the words and the way Shorty had delivered them. She picked up her coffee, burning her lips, but savouring the distraction.

'I told you I had a son, right?'

'You mentioned him a couple of times,' said Shorty, smiling. '*Hector*, right?'

'That's right,' said Erica, a small smile appearing on her face. There was something about Shorty that she dug. He was good-looking, had money from what she remembered, and he seemed like a decent guy. Even something as simple as making her a coffee had appealed to her. She'd had a few terrible relationships since she'd split up with Mori, and found she missed having someone around. Someone she could lean on.

'Can I tell you something?' Shorty said, after they'd sat in silence for a while.

'Okay . . . I'm a bit worried now, though,' Erica admitted, her eyebrows contracting. She braced herself for the bad news. She should have known it was too good to be true. He no doubt had a girlfriend that he loved; *last night was a terrible mistake. He would go back to her, and they would live happily ever after.* Erica felt nauseous now. The potent concoction of excessive alcohol and concern swirled around her stomach.

'The truth is . . . I kinda know you.'

'From where? I think I'd remember seeing you,' said Erica, frowning. Shorty shook his head.

'Seriously. I'm from the Hood, and we have people in common. Specifically, Hector's dad.'

'You know Mori?' she quickly asked, her stomach plummeting again. Mori had probably sent him to test her. Although they hadn't lasted long beyond Erica telling him she was pregnant, Mori had threatened multiple guys that had been around her, even hospitalising one.

'We're not close, but I know him.'

'Okay, so why are you telling me? I don't know what you heard, but we're not a thing anymore. He's my baby father, and that's it.'

Shorty nodded. 'I know. He's a piece of shit. He owes me and my friends some money.'

'Shit,' muttered Erica. It was just like Mori to make his problems hers. 'Look, I can't help you. I don't have any money, and—'

'I know, Erica. It's not like that. We know what he's like, and we know he doesn't pay you what he should pay towards his child . . . Especially with you doing all the work.'

Erica agreed, but she was still suspicious. 'What do you need me from me?'

Shorty took a deep breath, licking his lips and shifting forward on the sofa.

'Mori's been ducking us, but you can get him here. If you do, we can get the money he owes us, and then . . .'

'Then what?' Erica pressed.

'Then maybe we can get to know one another. This time without getting so drunk you can't remember things.' Shorty grinned.

Erica sighed, hesitating.

'Look, Mori is a really bad guy. He's already threatened me about bothering him. I don't know how well you know him, but he's killed people before. Maybe you should let this go.'

Shorty reached out, taking her hand in his.

'I won't force you into anything, but understand that I won't let Mori get to you. He talks tough, but he's avoiding me and my people for a reason. I can protect you, but I need your help first.' Shorty looked into Erica's eyes, pausing for a second. 'Trust me, babe.'

Erica considered what Shorty had said for a moment, tears pooling in her eyes. This was her chance to be free of Mori. To seek the sanctuary of a new partner. One who could truly provide for her and her son. It would cost her little. A small gesture; a token of sacrifice that she was more than willing to give. Wiping her tears away with the back of her hand, she smiled and nodded.

'Okay, Shorty. I'll help you.'

CHAPTER THIRTY-TWO

THE NEXT EVENING, Shorty sat with Erica. Hector sat on his mother's lap, lying horizontally along her legs, looking up at her with wide brown eyes. Erica looked down at her son with warmth and love.

Leaning back on the sofa and stretching his arm out, Shorty glanced across at Mori's child. He was a cute kid, he thought. He was small, with chubby cheeks and curly black hair that matched his dark eyes.

Shorty felt guilty for a moment, but quashed the feeling. Hector lost his chance at a proper family a long time ago. *Removing Mori from the picture entirely would make things simpler for Hector*, he reasoned.

Shorty sipped the rest of the coffee he'd made earlier. He was getting used to Erica's place. It was small, but homely, and his initial unease about being there had slowly ebbed away. Erica had done the best with what she had. Mori's generosity and government payments were her only source of income. She had no drive or ambition to work and make something for herself, which baffled Shorty. He hated being in debt or dependent on people. What he had, he'd made for himself.

AMBUSH

Stacey was the same. She had always been willing to go out and get her own money. She didn't mind splashing his, but didn't insist on it. Consequently, he tended to be looser with his purse strings.

As Shorty considered Stacey, he wondered what she was up to. He hadn't spoken to her much, and he expected her to be increasingly annoyed with his absence. Stacey knew the score and not to push things when Shorty needed space. This was business, and Shorty's role was important. His heart skipped when he remembered where he was, and he found himself hoping Stacey would never find out. He had done his best to minimise contact with Erica, but he was keen not to spook her. It was a fine line, and he was trying hard to stay the right side of it.

Putting those thoughts aside, Shorty cleared his throat, getting Erica's attention. She kept bouncing Hector on her lap, and the child giggled, enjoying the moment with his mother.

'Let's go over this one more time,' he said, ignoring the squeals of excitement. 'The plan is to get Mori here. That means when you ring him, you need to sound the part. He needs to believe something's wrong with Hector. Got it?'

'Yeah,' said Erica, wincing when Hector tugged on her hair. She was nervous and struggling to hide it. The plan seemed more intense the more she thought about it. It was a little closer to Mori's world than she expected. 'Do we need to involve my son, though?'

'Yes,' Shorty replied patiently. 'Mori needs to think there's trouble; his son is the only thing that will get him here.'

'He doesn't care about his son,' Erica grumbled, scowling. 'He doesn't care about anyone but himself.'

'I don't believe that,' said Shorty.

'I know him better than you do. I had his kid.' Erica huffed.

'Still. He gives you money for his son.'

'Not much,' Erica argued.

'That's not the point,' said Shorty. 'It's proof he at least cares about his son.' He could tell from Erica's face that she wanted to argue some more. When he smiled at her, she visibly relaxed. 'Everything's gonna be fine. I promise. You don't need to be scared.'

'I know . . . it's just, he's a lot, you know?'

'I know, but don't worry,' said Shorty. He looked at his watch, then grabbed his phone. 'Let's get started.' He dialled Marcus's number. 'Yo, it's me. Come by the spot. Bring K-Bar with you too. Okay, cool.' Hanging up, Shorty put his phone on the coffee table.

A feeling of foreboding spread through Erica's body, and she couldn't ignore it.

'Why do we need so many people?' she asked, raising a questioning eyebrow. 'I'm not sure how I feel about you bringing strangers into my house.' By now, Hector had fallen quiet, and she knew he was getting tired.

'Do you trust me?' Shorty stared deeply into her eyes. Erica hesitated, and Shorty picked up on it. 'If you don't, then we're fucked before we even begin. We need trust to see this through.'

'I'm sorry,' said Erica, sighing. 'It's just Mori . . .' she trailed off. Shorty shifted closer.

'I get it. I'm not inviting my boys round to make you feel uncomfortable. It's more security, meaning there's no chance Mori will get away without paying what he owes. No chance of him losing his temper and hurting somebody.' Shorty's eyes flicked between Erica and her son. 'Okay?'

Erica smiled again, reassured.

'Okay, Shorty. I trust you.'

When Shorty's friends arrived, though, Erica found her fears returning. K-Bar, a slender, dreadlocked man she was sure she had seen around before, was polite, but distant.

Marcus, the man Shorty had rung, was the biggest, most imposing man she had ever seen. He was over-muscled and had a dangerous look about him. It was easy for Erica to see why Shorty would want him on board as security.

'Would you like anything to drink?' She asked them. K-Bar shook his head, and Marcus ignored her completely. 'Right . . . I'll put this little man to bed,' she said in a falsely upbeat voice. Shorty gave her a small smile, but no one else spoke. As soon as Erica left the room, they began talking.

Erica took Hector to his room and put him in his cot. He fussed a little, but didn't wake up. She stared at him for a few moments, enjoying how peaceful he looked. *She was doing this for him*, she told herself. With the money she would get, she and Hector would be okay, and if Mori said anything, then Shorty and his friends would protect her.

Taking a deep breath, she stood a few minutes later and headed back downstairs.

Whatever conversation had taken place between the three men had ended by the time she returned. K-Bar had planted himself against the wall. Marcus was pacing the room, though he paused when he saw her. Shorty remained in the same place, looking relaxed.

'Make the call. Now,' Marcus said to her in a rough voice. Erica shot him a scornful look, buoyed by Shorty's presence.

'Oi, this is my house. Don't come in here and start giving me orders.'

'Chill, people,' Shorty interjected, before Marcus could reply. He patted the seat next to him, and Erica sat, giving Marcus one last look, not liking the hard-eyed glare he was shooting back at her. 'It's cool,' Shorty continued. 'Don't worry about Marcus. Stick to the plan, and everything will be fine.'

Erica hugged him, reassured by his muscular arms. He gave her a hug and a small kiss. 'Make the call now, please.'

Nodding, Erica grabbed her phone and called Mori.

'What the fuck do you want?' he snapped when he answered. 'I'm busy.'

'Too busy for your son?'

'What the hell does that mean?'

'It means that Hector is ill,' she said, injecting panic into her voice. 'He's been coughing all day, and now he won't stop throwing up. His face is blue and I don't know what's wrong with him,'

'Shit. What the hell have you done to him? Call a damn ambulance.'

'I need you here, Mori. I don't know what to do,' her voice rose. She heard him curse on the other end.

'Fuck. Right, I'm on my way. If you've messed up my son, I'm gonna cut you into little pieces, you fucking idiot.' Mori hung up, and Erica took a deep breath. She wiped away the tears that had formed in her eyes, embarrassed that they'd heard how Mori spoke to her. Shorty put his arm around her and pulled her close.

'You did well,' he murmured, before turning to his associates. 'You two, wait upstairs in Hector's room. I'll hide down here just in case.'

Marcus took out a baggie of cocaine, sprinkling some on the back of his hand and sniffing, his head jolting as his eyes closed. Erica glanced at Shorty, whose expression was blank.

'You want some?' Marcus offered the small bag to K-Bar.

'No thanks.' K-Bar glanced at Erica, but added nothing else. Marcus shrugged and stowed his bag of drugs. He and K-Bar both had gloves on. Erica hadn't even noticed. She looked to Shorty, and noted he now had on a pair, wondering where they'd come from.

Marcus and K-Bar headed upstairs. Erica's worries grew again, her heart racing.

'Are you sure about this?' she whispered to Shorty, who nodded.

'Everything's gonna be fine. Trust me. Hector couldn't be any safer with them. He's gonna be protected, no matter what goes down.'

AMBUSH

Erica didn't want to consider what such a statement meant, so she pressed herself closer to Shorty and tried to ignore her heart catapulting against her chest.

———

Mori drove to Erica's at speed, furious and growing ever more nervous about his son. His baby mother sounded vague on the phone, and Mori's first assumption was that her negligence had impacted his son. She would pay if that was the case.

Mori wasn't a fool. He knew she used his money for things other than Hector. He knew all about her shopping trips and wild nights out with her useless friends. The day he'd let her trap him was a day he would forever regret.

Switching lanes sharply, Mori ignored a driver hammering on his horn behind him. Looking into his rear-view mirror, he saw the man's face, reddening with rage.

Putting his foot down, he sped away from the car behind, focusing on his son. He couldn't help but feel guilty. He'd spent little time with his Hector. He gave Erica money to take care of him, but knew it wasn't enough.

Mori had grown up in a broken household himself, and he understood what impact that could have on a child. With his own dad abandoning him, being a father was not something that came naturally to Mori. He struggled to relate to Hector, but he regretted that he hadn't tried harder.

As he got closer to the house, Mori made up his mind. He would be more present in Hector's life. He would be the dad that Mori never had. The thought of cooperating with Erica angered him, though. Hector being sick was no doubt her fault, and he would ensure she was punished for whatever she had done to him.

For a moment, Mori wondered if he and his son could make it alone. Removing Erica from the situation would make things less complex and, as long as he could commit his time, his son would probably benefit.

The situation with Marcus was a complication. Mori had a distant Aunt who lived out of the way in Shadwell. He could pay her to look after Hector until the drama was over. Mori kissed his teeth as he further considered his Aunt. He was sick of the women in his life fleecing his money, but he was willing to do what was necessary.

He shelved his thoughts as he pulled up outside Erica's place. The street was empty, but he could hear a dog barking in the distance. He glanced at his gun on the passenger seat, but decided to leave it. He wanted to be responsible around Hector now, and didn't want to fall at the first hurdle.

Rushing up the path, he hammered on the front door, forcing his way past Erica, missing the stricken look on her face.

'Where's my son?' he demanded.

'He's upstairs, but—'

'He better be okay, you stupid bitch. You'd better have called that ambulance too.' Mori hurried up the stairs and rushed into his son's room. He got a split-second glance at Hector sleeping peacefully in his cot. Mori heard the movement, and before he could act, two men were all over him. He struggled, but they had the drop on him. He quickly recognised them as Marcus and K-Bar, just as Marcus drove his fist into Mori's stomach.

Mori fell to his knees, gasping for air as the pair held him down. Mori didn't struggle. It was futile. They were far too strong.

He heard more footsteps as Erica and a man he recognised as Shorty rushed up the stairs and into the room.

'You set me up, you fucking bitch,' Mori snarled, straining to glare at his baby mother.

'It's not my fault,' Erica hissed, not wanting to wake Hector. 'You should have paid them what you owe them.'

AMBUSH

Mori shot her a scornful look, his head pressed into the carpet, just before Marcus lifted him to his feet.

'You're so fucking daft. I don't owe them money. They're here to kill me.'

Erica's eyes widened.

'No . . . That's . . . it's not true,' she stammered.

'Get him out of here,' Marcus ordered. Shorty and K-Bar dragged Mori down the stairs and out of the house, securing him in the back of the car Marcus and K-Bar had driven in.

In the house, Erica glared at Marcus.

'You lot are fucking foul for lying to me,' she snapped, hearing Hector stir. 'I want the money you promised me, or I'm not staying quiet. Trust me on that.' Erica folded her arms, her face contorted in defiant frustration.

Marcus frowned as he met her gaze. Taking out his gun, he aimed it at her chest and fired. The sound of the silenced gun pinged around the room, seemingly bouncing from wall to wall. As Erica's body hit the floor, Hector awoke. Pulling himself up on the wooden cot, he stared down at his mother, gurgling.

Erica was still. Her mouth was open, a perfect picture of shock that Marcus had captured eternally. He glanced down at her, shooting her again, before leaving.

CHAPTER THIRTY-THREE

MARCUS DIDN'T RUSH BACK to the car. He had no reason to. When people rushed about after doing dirt, they usually drew more attention to themselves. He kept his head down and climbed into the passenger seat. K-Bar was behind the wheel, and he pulled off immediately.

Marcus glanced at Mori in the rearview mirror. He expected him to be all force and fire, making threats, but he seemed downcast. Defeated. Shorty had secured his hands and had a gun on him, just in case he tried something.

'Did you kill her?' Mori asked after a few moments, his voice hoarse.

Marcus didn't respond.

Mori sighed, nodding.

'I get it. I'd have done the same thing. She's mouthy. No matter what deal you made, she wouldn't have stuck to it. Never should have breeded her.' Mori didn't speak for a moment. 'Hector . . . my son. Did you . . .?'

'I wouldn't hurt a kid,' said Marcus, scowling.

'Good. That's good. Thanks.'

No one spoke. The car steadily hugged the roads. Marcus was content with the silence. He had one more loose end to tie up, then the situation was over. He could go back to his normal life, having righted the wrong. Marcus heard Mori sniffle, but paid it no attention.

'It was business, Marcus. I went at you, and you went at me. I took out your people. You took out mine. Why can't we make a deal?'

Marcus didn't respond. Mori gave it a few seconds before he tried again.

'I can help you. All of you. Wisdom is sitting on some serious money. I'm tight with him. I can help you get it. We don't even have to split it. It can just be my tax. Me and my son will get out of Leeds and never return. No one has to know any different.'

Marcus wasn't making a deal with Mori. The die had been cast the moment he'd attempted to have Marcus killed. From that point, they had been on a collision course that would only end with death.

'I know what you're thinking,' Mori said hurriedly, his panic growing. 'I'm not gonna snake you. I don't even want revenge. I just want to live with my son . . .' Mori began crying now. Full-on sobs. Marcus still didn't react, but knew that he and the other occupants in the car were thinking the same thing. Mori was completely broken. He'd likely been on the other end many times; leading someone to their doom, ignoring their attempts to bargain for their lives.

Now the shoe was on the other foot. He was the one begging for his life. He was the one crying and snivelling.

If only the streets could see him now, Marcus thought to himself. He'd expected Mori to fight his way out. To go down swinging in a blaze of glory. He couldn't have been more wrong. He had given up the second Marcus and K-Bar had laid hands on him. He understood his fate and that it was his time.

Finally, the car pulled to a stop. Mori was still weeping. Marcus exited, then waited for Shorty and K-Bar to drag Mori from the car. They'd driven just outside a patch of woods, miles away from the Hood. Marcus led the way as Mori was pulled along.

Shorty and K-Bar forced him to his knees after they'd been walking for nearly ten minutes. Marcus strode across to a tree, removing a purple ribbon that had been wrapped around it, and placing it in his pocket. Beside the tree was a deep ditch, that Sharma and Victor had diligently dug earlier. The area had been swept. Despite the hole, there were no other signs of their presence. It was an impressive job.

Marcus walked across to the hole, placing his hands on one of two shovels and leaning on it. Shorty and K-Bar hung back, letting Marcus have his moment. Standing up straight, he pulled his gun out, aiming it at Mori. Marcus met his eyes, seeing a single tear trace down Mori's cheek.

Marcus shook his head. He was disappointed with Mori. How he had given up and the weakness he had shown since they captured him. It left a bitter-sweet taste in Marcus's mouth. A hollow victory.

'Marcus . . .'

'Shut up. Wisdom. What did he know? And did he help you?'

Mori blinked helplessly, another tear escaping his eye. Marcus stepped closer, pressing the gun into Mori's face.

'Answer the question.'

'W-Wisdom was . . . helping me,' Mori said, sobbing.

Tilting his head to the side, Marcus squeezed the trigger, the crack ricocheting around the woods. Mori slumped backwards, a hole in the middle of his face. Marcus fired twice more.

When they finished, Marcus took a deep breath. It felt like the saga had dragged on forever, but he'd finally finished Mori.

The police would likely conduct an investigation. Marcus assumed they would pay more attention to Erica's death than the others, but Mori had been right. Leaving her alive had never been an option.

Mori likely still had allies out there, but Marcus would be ready for them if they tried it. If they were smart, they'd keep their mouths shut and let the matter die. Wisdom was another matter. He had helped Mori go after him. Marcus's assumptions had been proven. He would need to speak to Lamont and give him the lay of the land.

'Are we done?' Shorty asked after a few moments.

'Yeah. We'll stop at a phone box on the way back and call in what happened to Mori's woman. No need for the kid to suffer unnecessarily.' For a fleeting second, Marcus wondered who would look after the child, then instantly dismissed it. It wasn't his problem.

'Come on then,' said Shorty. 'Let's jet. L and that other prick will wanna know what's gone down.'

After rolling Mori's body into the ditch and covering it thoroughly, the trio left, Shorty and K-Bar holding the shovels over their shoulders.

EPILOGUE

SEVERAL DAYS LATER, Marcus and Lamont met at Lamont's house. They sat in the back garden, looking out at the sky. The weather was fairly warm for winter, and they both sat comfortably in t-shirts.

'Any static?' Lamont asked. He wasn't one for company, but had a sturdy table in his back garden, and several comfortable wooden chairs. Most of the time, they remained covered to combat the elements, but he found it nice to sit outside and ponder things every once in a while.

'Not really. We've stayed out of the spotlight so far. Everyone knows, and as we guessed, most of the static is centred around Mori's dead baby mother,' said Marcus. 'We left Mori's car out front. He's copping the blame for the murder. Word is that he's still on the run.'

Lamont made a face. Marcus knew what he was going to say before the words left his mouth.

'Did you have to kill his baby mother?'

'Yes,' said Marcus. 'Don't forget, it was your idea to use her in the first place.'

'I said to use her to track him down. I said nothing about killing her,' Lamont retorted.

AMBUSH

'She saw all of us. Shorty wasn't gonna be able to keep her sweet forever. She wasn't bothered about Mori, but she was greedy enough to hold it over our heads if she didn't get what she wanted. Just before I popped her, she was already talking about the feds,' said Marcus.

Lamont sighed. Marcus knew he still wasn't happy about the situation, but he understood it was necessary.

'So what next then?' Lamont asked.

'You tell me, boss,' Marcus responded.

Lamont looked at Marcus for a moment, scratching his chin.

'Run me through it again. What did Mori say?'

'I asked him if Wisdom was involved. If he was backing Mori. He told me he was. I don't think we will get anything more clean cut than that,' said Marcus.

Lamont continued to stare ahead.

'You remember our arrangement?' Marcus asked when Lamont didn't respond. Lamont turned to look at his friend, nodding slightly.

'I do,' he said.

'So you know what I have to do?'

Again, Lamont nodded.

'Just be patient, though. Let me speak to Wisdom first. We will go from there.'

'Ok, blood. Sounds good,' Marcus said, smiling.

'So what are you going to do now?' Lamont asked, rising to his feet. Marcus did the same.

'Go home. Take a shower and get some food,' Marcus replied. Slapping hands, the pair embraced.

'Yeah, you go get that shower, bro,' Lamont said as he backed up, his top lip curled.

'Man, fuck you,' said Marcus, laughing.

'I'll get at you later, bro,' said Lamont, turning and going inside.

Marcus left. Heading home, he went into the kitchen,

rummaging around his cupboards until he found what he was looking for; a large block of cocaine. Collapsing onto the sofa, he switched on the television, chopping out multiple lines. One by one, he inhaled them, watching as a news reporter gesticulated wildly in front of Erica's house.

Marcus placed his note on the table, mind spinning as he focused on the blue and white crime scene tape rippling behind her.

―――

Chink knocked on Angie's door, smiling when Georgia answered. She beamed at him, her eyes twinkling with happiness.

'Hey, Xiyu. It's great to see you. Come in.'

Chink shook his head. 'It's just a flyby visit,' he said. Georgia tensed, worried he was going to give her some bad news.

'What's happened, Xiyu? Please, just tell me.'

'It's over,' said Chink. 'The problem has been taken care of. You can go home now.'

Without thinking, Georgia felt her eyes tearing up. She flung her arms around Chink, pressing against his chest, inhaling the smell of him, feeling him wrap his arms around her for a moment.

'What happened?'

Chink shook his head.

'Nothing major. It was all worked out. These things always are in the end. No one's going to come after you.'

'Did you help?' Georgia suddenly asked. 'You know . . .with sorting things out?'

Chink smiled at her again as she stepped away from his frame.

'I mean, I don't like to brag . . . but I kind of masterminded the entire plan,' Chink said, smiling playfully and brushing his shoulder.

Georgia kissed him on the cheek, her lips lingering for a second.

'Thank you,' she told him.

'You don't need to thank me.' Chink took a deep breath. 'There's something else you need to know. It's about Marcus.'

Fear cascaded through Georgia again, just as she'd let her guard down. Her hands shook as terror overcame her.

'Is he hurt?'

'He's hurting himself,' said Chink.

'What does that mean?'

'It means that he has a drug problem, and it's getting out of hand.'

'No . . .' Georgia shook her head. 'I live with him. I'd know—'

Did you know he's borrowed money from me in the past? Tens of thousands of pounds? Where's it going if it's not up his nose?' Chink asked. 'I'm not trying to be insensitive, forgive me. I care about Marcus and I don't want to see him hurt. I think he would lose it if he found out I'd told you what I suspect, but what can I do? Just stand and watch him kill himself?' Chink was breathless, looking past Georgia. After a moment, he met her eyes. 'He's taken thousands of pounds worth of drugs from me, Georgia. He needs help.'

Georgia's mouth fell open as she tried to process what Xiyu had said to her.

'Why . . . why are you telling me this?'

'Because you deserved to know, Georgia. You deserve the truth and honesty. And if you didn't get that, you wouldn't be able to help him,' Chink said to her. 'Hopefully, I'll see you around. If you need anything, you know how to get in touch with me.'

Chink left her on the doorstep as he headed down the drive. Climbing into his car, he started the engine, chancing a glance back at Georgia. Seeing her still standing there, mouth wide open, he smiled and pulled away.

Wisdom was already sitting on a park bench as Lamont approached. He stuck his hands in the pockets of his coat, attempting to combat the biting wind. Lamont took a seat beside Wisdom, both of them staring straight ahead.

Only a few people were out in the park. Two elderly Asian men were walking around the path, talking to one another in steady tones. A man with a protruding stomach in grey jogging bottoms tossed a stick for his dog to catch, already looking over-exerted from the effort.

Lamont watched them in silence. He was calm and collected but could sense a different energy in Wisdom. Lamont waited him out, continuing to stare ahead. He had come alone, which impressed Lamont. He had expected Sonny Black to accompany him. A show of strength and intent, but he didn't.

'Did you come here to say nothing?' Wisdom finally spoke, his tone as biting as the weather.

'I figured I'd wait for you to speak,' replied Lamont. 'I imagine there are some things you want to get off your chest.'

'That's it?' That's all you have to say?'

'Mori's gone. There's nothing else for me to say.'

'Bullshit,' Wisdom hissed, all composure forgotten. 'Our joint aim has always been peace, L. We do business in the right way, and we make money and look after the people around us. Nowhere in that does it state that we kill innocent women and leave their kids parentless.'

'Mori started it,' Lamont reminded him. 'He decided of his own accord to engage in a battle with the most dangerous man in Chapeltown, and he paid the price.'

Wisdom shook his head. 'What happened was a violation, L. There have to be repercussions.'

Lamont turned to Wisdom and smiled.

'You want to talk about violations? Mori told us, Wisdom.'

Panic struck Wisdom's face.

'What do you mean?'

'You knew. All along. You helped him. You weren't brokering for peace, you were buying time. We know you provided support for Mori. There's no point in denying it,' Lamont said.

A silence engulfed the pair who sat, staring at one another. When Wisdom's mouth opened, Lamont held his hand up, continuing.

'Explain to me how that is a peaceful act, Wisdom. Marcus is my brother, and you tried to have him taken out.'

'You're jumping to conclusions, Lamont. There's a lot more to this than meets the eye.'

Lamont shrugged, sliding to his feet. 'That's possible. It's in your best interests to let this go,' he said. 'If you want to escalate matters, please understand it won't just be Marcus you're running against.'

With his message delivered, Lamont walked away, leaving Wisdom staring after him.

ALSO BY RICKY BLACK

The Target Series:

Origins: The Road To Power

Target

Target Part 2: The Takedown

Target Part 3: Absolute Power

The Complete Target Series Boxset

The Deeds Family Series:

Blood & Business

Good Deeds, Bad Deeds

Deeds to the City

Hustler's Ambition

No More Deeds

Other books by Ricky Black:

Homecoming

ABOUT RICKY BLACK

Ricky Black was born and raised in Chapeltown, Leeds.

In 2016, he published the first of his crime series, Target, and has published thirteen more books since.

Visit https://rickyblackbooks.com for information regarding new releases and special offers, and promotions.

Copyright © 2023 by Ricky Black

All rights reserved.

No part of this book may be reproduced in any form or by any electronic or mechanical means, including information storage and retrieval systems, without written permission from the author, except for the use of brief quotations in a book review.

Printed in Great Britain
by Amazon